PLAY

She was hiding
heady perfume so
A chalky moonlig
she was materialised. She stood there like a figure in a charade – little girl lost. Like one of the frightened phantoms of her lonely childhood.

He lit a cigarette to calm his screaming nerves. 'Evelyn, what do you want?'

'David, please . . . ' Her voice was like a telephoned whisper – distorted and unrecognisable.

'Evelyn, let me take you home.'

Her head snapped up, the eyes wild. 'I'm going to stay here, David. You're going to make love to me tonight, whether you want to or not. And you're going to do it again in the future, if I want you to. I'm with you for the duration. You are not – repeat, not – going to dump me.'

Then, suddenly, she was smiling that sweet, little-girl smile again, her eyes innocent of threat or jealousy.

And the nightmare terror slipped back into the shadows.

PLAY MISTY FOR ME

Paul J. Gillette

A STAR BOOK
published by
the Paperback Division of
W. H. ALLEN & Co. PLC

A Star Book
First published in Great Britain in Tandem by
Universal-Tandem Publishing Co. Ltd, 1972
Reprinted in 1978, 1980, 1982, 1985
by the Paperback Division of
W. H. Allen & Co. PLC
44 Hill Street, London W1X 8LB

First published in the United States by Universal Publishing
and
Distributing Corporation, 1971

Based on the screenplay by Jo Heims and Dean Riesner;
story by Jo Heims

Printed and bound in Great Britain by
Anchor Brendon Ltd, Tiptree, Essex

ISBN 0 352 30273 9

Dedication
to
Mike Saurino

ONE

The cliffs rose out of the water like great, hulking football linemen massed to defend a passer against red-dogging waves.

Standing on top of them, with the echo of the breakers filling your ears and a few thousand miles of ocean stretching out in front of you, you could get the feeling that you were alone on a pedestal-like island. If you tried hard enough, you might even persuade yourself that you and your island were all that existed.

Dave Garland stared out at the ocean and wished he could persuade himself that Tobie Williams didn't exist, or at least talk himself into accepting that it was all over between them and that it was useless to torture himself by chasing her memory all over town.

Fat chance. She was more with him in her absence

than she ever had been in her presence. She was, to borrow from his favorite poet, with him evermore.

Tobie Williams. The girl he had taken for granted. Like morning coffee. Or that the gas station guy will come running to fill your tank whenever you pull up to his pumps. Oh well, so much for unwarranted assumptions. A bird in the hand, to switch from Poe to Plutarch, may fly away any day.

Dave Garland stared down at the waves breaking against the rocks. The balcony on which he stood—Tobie Williams' balcony—was built over the palisades, with only a weather-beaten railing of two-by-fours protecting its occupants from the great beyond. Lean over too far, or let the railing suddenly give way, and that would be the end of it.

Dave Garland wondered what it would feel like to plummet over the edge. Probably you'd hang in space for a moment that seemed like forever; then you'd feel the bottom fall out from under you, and you'd hurtle toward the rocks, down, down, watching them grow larger and larger as they drew nearer and nearer at—what was the free-fall rate of acceleration he had learned in high school physics class?—thirty-two feet per second/per second? Yes, that was it: thirty-two the first second, sixty-four the next, one hundred and twenty-eight the third, and so on . . .

Until?

Splat! A monstrous black-gray rock covered with blood and flesh and shattered bone.

And then?

Well, since the house was all boarded up and Tobie

was who-knows-where, the body wouldn't be discovered right away. Meanwhile, the waves would batter against the rock every minute of every day, each one taking some of the debris with it, until, finally, in the not-too-distant future, all traces would be gone.

The thought made Dave Garland shudder. Instinctively he stepped back from the rail.

What, he asked himself, *are you doing here?*

There was, of course, no answer. At least, there was no answer which ordinary mortals would accept. But a poet would understand.

What had Poe written?

Thou wast that all to me, love,
For which my soul did pine—.
A green isle in the sea, love,
A fountain and a shrine,
All wreathed with fairy fruits and flowers,
And all the flowers were mine . . .

[Now] all my days are trances,
And all my nightly dreams
Are where thy gray eye glances,
And where thy footstep gleams—

Yes, Poe, as usual, had the answers. And that, along with twenty-five cents, would get you a hamburger at McDonald's.

Dave Garland squinted against the wind as the customary early-evening fog moved in from the sea. Tobie Williams: his one and only love. The only problem was, he had never bothered to tell her. Maybe because he didn't realize how much she meant to him until she was gone. Glutton that he was, he had to have his cake and eat it, too. One girl wasn't enough. Not for Dave Garland. Not for the Big D.

Love, for the Big D, was a four-letter word: MORE.

Now, now, David, don't be too harsh on yourself. She, after all, drove you to it. If it weren't for her hang-up—that incessant, overpowering fear of commitment, as evidenced by that never-ending parade of roommates—you wouldn't have been compelled to play the field. . . .

Of course, if you had demonstrated *your* commitment first—if you, say, had asked her to m-a-r-r-y you instead of merely to move in with you. . . .

But that, in this day and age, was ridiculous. How could a man know he wanted to marry a woman until he had lived with her?

Still—

Oh, shit! This kind of thinking is ridiculous!

Dave turned from the sea and climbed the three stairs leading from Tobie Williams' balcony to the catwalk behind her house. Overlooking the balcony was a huge, floor-to-ceiling picture window; through it Dave could see the spacious, rustic living room where he and Tobie had spent so many happy hours way-back-when. Now all the furniture was covered with sheets, and the only hint of what the living room used to be like was the huge portrait over the fireplace: the portrait she had painted of Dave.

Shit!!!

He followed the catwalk to the corner of the house, where a gravel path led to the driveway and his MG. As he neared the driveway he heard the car radio and remembered that he had left the motor running.

"Seven thirty-two in the blue, blue, blue of the evening, and this is Al Monte here talkin' just to you from clear-channel radio, KRML, Carmel, California. Now here's The Revival with some stone swamp rock—"

Dave reached the car just as a sheriff's sedan pulled into the driveway, blocking his exit. "You lost?" a uniformed deputy asked.

Dave made himself smile. "Not exactly."

"Well?" The deputy leaned against the MG and hitched up his pants *à la* Rod Steiger in *In the Heat of the Night*. "Don't tell me you came all the way out here just to watch the fog come in."

"A friend of mine used to live here."

"Nobody living here now. It's been closed up for three months."

"Closer to four," Dave said.

The deputy seemed not to hear him. "We're supposed to keep an eye on these places, make sure nobody—" He stopped suddenly, and his brow furrowed. "Hey, aren't you Dave Garland?"

"That's right."

"Wow, whatcha doin' out here, Dave?" From Rod

Steiger to Petey Punk in four and a half seconds. He looked at his watch. "You're gonna have to haul ass if you wanna make it into Carmel by eight."

"I'm not gonna make it anywhere if you don't get your car out of the driveway."

"Sure, Dave. Right away." The deputy retreated to his sedan. "Be list'nin' for ya. Nice talkin' to ya."

Dave waited until the way was clear, then rammed his gearshift into low and, kicking up gravel, tore out of the driveway and onto the access road to the coastal highway.

It was a cool night, and the wind against his face felt good. Somehow, when he was at the wheel of the MG, top down, driving a little too fast, everything was okay; no worries, no hassles—and he didn't think of Tobie at all . . .

. . . except, of course, when he glanced at the glove compartment knob, now bare of the litter bag she always used to hang over it. Good old ecologically oriented Tobe, one of the Earth People back in the days when what now passes for Earth People were littering beaches with their beer cans.

. . . or when he checked the rear-view mirror for cops and remembered how she always used to do the fuzz-watch for him. Good ol' eagle-eye Tobe, spot one of the bastards from forty-miles-of-bad-road away.

Forty Miles of Bad Road? Now where did that one come from? Fifty-seven? Fifty-eight? Sometime back then. An instrumental. The Ventures. Or somebody. Maybe Duane Eddie. Anyway, it was from back in the days when the Big D was doing his thing on little daytime five thousand watters out in the sticks, playing Top Forty crap and sneaking in what poetry he could by making jokes about it . . .

A loaf of bread, a jug of wine, and thou
Beside me in the wilderness—oh, wow!
BOINGGGG! ! ! Chime-time at the tone, folks, two
and a quarter past. . . Here's the Five Satins . . .

Where was Tobie Williams then? And if one was capable of surviving without her at that time (way back when one was not even aware of her existence) why not now?

Yes, why not?

"Neil Diamond," Al Monte fake-enthused in that stereotypical Top Forty deejay's voice, "showing up on the charts with a fast-breaking single on the Uni-label. Nineteen from now it'll be the Big D, Dave Garland, here with a little Poe and a lot mo'. Meanwhile you're ridin' the range with the Italian stallion . . ."

Dave Garland drove by the Bixby Bridge and remembered the time he and Tobie Williams had driven out at four in the morning to watch the cops rescue the guy that had phoned the radio station saying he was going to jump, and remembered how, after the crowd had all left, he and she had stood there watching the sunrise and being very much aware of their love for each other, and beginning to believe that it would never end . . .

. . . and that's why, even though one was capable

of surviving very nicely without her way-back-when, it became increasingly difficult here-and-now.

I get along without you very well,
Except, of course . . .

Thank you, Mister Sinatra. You do a torch song like no one ever has and no one ever will.

Torch song!? Where did that expression come from? Nineteen forty-six?

Now, now, Dave, you're not *that* old. Matter of fact, you were only a child in forty-six.

Ah yes, but everybody else who's around nowadays was waiting on line to get born in nineteen forty-six!

Forty-six: come to think of it, the year of Tobie Williams' birth.

Shit! Is there no escape?

Dave drove past Hurricane Point. "And here's one," Al Monte was saying, "from the funk capital of the world—Mitch Corday did it at Staff Recording Studios in Arlington, Vee-ay—that stands for Virginia, momma . . ."

Dave pressed down on the accelerator. Pick up a little more speed, work a little harder at driving, think about Tobie Williams a little less . . .

Fat chance.

An' I'll be tryin'
To forget chew,
But try as I may . . .

Johnny Sacca and the Hilltoppers? Jimmy Sacca? Stevie Sacca?

Fifty-five? No, fifty-four. Or fifty-three?

Shit!

Dave pulled off the coastal highway and navigated a sharp turn onto Carmel's scenic seaside road. "The time," said Al Monte, "is seven and seven-times-seven—yes, momma, seven forty-nine. The temperature is a great sixty-eight. And daddy, take out the grog—cause the weatherman says . . . fog!"

Foggy day,
London town,
Had me low,
Had me down—Anita O'Day inflection, just right for the mood now . . .

Oh, damn it, Tobie, why are we doing this to each other?

Or . . .

. . . to narrow it down to proper perspective . . .

. . . why are you doing this to me?

(Why am I *letting* you do this to me?)

(Why am *I* doing this to me?)

Oh, shit.

"Wrapping it up for this week," said Al Monte, "some Blood, some Sweat, and some Tears . . ."

Dave tromped on his brakes and pulled to a squealing halt in the parking space with his name on it behind the two-story building labeled STATION KRML, in a shopping center which could have been located anywhere from BeautifulDowntownBurbank to MarvelousMidtownMiami but happened, as it were, to be located in CheerfulCentralCarmel.

"And here he comes," said Al Monte, glancing up through the broadcast booth window and heaving a very visible sigh of relief as Dave entered the studio, "your friend and mine, the raven maven, Edgar Allan Garland, all ready to bring you five uninterrupted hours of mellow groove. So, sweet people, till next Monday this is the stallion sayin', hang in there, babies, because everything's gonna be just—everything!"

Dave tossed him a mock salute and went to the modest-sized office next to the booth. He riffled through a stack of mail someone had left on top of his desk and found an envelope with a San Francisco return address.

"One of these days, baby," said Al Monte, materializing at his shoulder, "you're gonna walk in here and find the big boss staring you in the eye and wanting to know why you weren't in the studio half an hour before airtime like it says in the little ol' rulebook. I mean, cutting it close is cutting it close, daddy, but wow!"

"Sorry, Al." Dave did not look up from the letter.

"No hassle for me, baby. I mean, *I* don't care what time you come in. I can always put on one of the old tapes I keep cued up in anticipation of your inevitable tardy arrival, and all the sweet folks out in radioland'll never know the difference. So—at the risk of sounding repetitious—why should *I* care what time you come in?

But Mister Big, baby—Mister Big won't look at it quite that way—" He suddenly noticed that Dave wasn't listening. Then he noticed the return address on the envelope, and his eyes widened. "The Frisco gig?"

Dave nodded.

"Is it definite?"

"Nope. They want some pictures and a biography. And another tape."

"What was wrong with the first one?"

Dave shrugged, then dropped the letter on his desk. He went to the record cabinet in the corner and began pulling albums and singles.

Al silently read the letter and did a double-take when he came to the signature. "Madge Brenner?"

"Yeah. She's putting it together."

"Well, break out the champagne, baby—you're as good as in."

"What makes you think so?"

Al smirked knowingly. "I heard stories about her when she was running KANG in L.A. They say part of a deejay's job was ringing her chimes."

"She's a fifty-five-year-old woman with grandchildren."

"When did that ever stop you, baby?"

Dave offered a Lascivious Young Gigolo grin as he stacked the records on top of his desk and began rummaging through a drawer full of poetry anthologies. "Cue up my theme, will you, baby?"

"Already did."

"You're a real human being."

"And you—" Al pointed to the large electric clock

inside the broadcast booth; the big red second-hand was approaching the twelve—"are on the air."

Dave went to the console, bled out Al Monte's theme, touched the switch triggering the taped call-letters announcement, then bled in his own theme. Quickly flipping to a premarked page in one of his anthologies, he read,

"I was a child and she was a child,
"In this kingdom by the sea,
"But we loved with a love that was more than love—
"I and my Annabel Lee. . . .
"Our love it was stronger by far than the love
"Of those who were older than we—
"Of many far wiser than we—
"And neither the angels in heaven above,
"Nor the demons down under the sea,
"Can ever dissever my soul from the soul
"Of the beautiful Annabel Lee."

He closed the book, then:

"Dave Garland back again to bring you a little talk, a line or two of verse, and five hours of music to be very, very nice to each other by."

He turned a dial that brought his theme up to full volume. Promptly the light on one of the phones began flashing.

"KRML, Dave Garland," he answered.

There was a pause, then a soft, familiar female voice. "Play *Misty* for me?"

"Be glad to." Dave scribbled the title on a notepad. "Thanks for calling."

"Thank you," she purred, hanging up.

Al Monte read the title. "The *Misty* chick again?"

Dave nodded.

"Wow, that's the third time this week. She must be on Errol Garner's payroll."

Dave cued up a lush, saxophone-rich ballad by Woody Herman's current herd, then cut his theme and touched a switch triggering a commercial from the tape deck.

"You know," Al continued, "you oughtta tell that chick to fall by some night and say hello. Who knows? If she has a pair of tits, she could help take your mind off the Tobe."

"Yeah," Dave replied absently. "Next time, maybe." The phone was flashing again. "KRML, Dave Garland."

TWO

The night wasn't forty hours long. It only seemed forty hours long. Finally, when Dave was beginning to believe that he might spend the rest of his life chained to the console, the studio door opened and Murray Black, the one-to-six ayem man, came in. Dave wrapped up his final segment, climbed wearily into the MG, and headed for the Sardine Factory.

The Factory was a saloon on Cannery Row—one of the nicer joints, more of a neighborhood bar than a tourist trap; a place where you could sit all night nursing one beer, if that was all you wanted, or drink until you passed out and be sure that someone would see to it that you got home. As usual at this time of night, it was nearly empty.

Dave went to the bulletin board at the corner of the

bar and glanced through the scraps of paper tacked there. None of the messages was for him.

He took a small address book from his pocket, riffled through it, marked a page with his finger, started toward the telephone at the opposite end of the bar, then changed his mind. He wasn't in the mood for one of the old standbys tonight. He wanted the One and Only. And she wasn't to be had.

He shoved the book back into his pocket and flopped down on the nearest stool. Almost immediately a bottle of beer materialized in front of him. Attached to the bottle was an arm, the upper half of which was covered with the sleeve of a modish blue shirt. The owner of the arm and the shirt—and the Sardine Factory—was a medium-tall, medium-heavy guy in his mid-forties who combed his graying hair sideways to camouflage a rapidly receding hairline. His name was Johnny Murphy.

"Heard the show," he said. "Makes a man wonder. Thirty G's a year, they pay you. And for what? Read a few poems, play a couple records. Sure as hell beats working for a living."

"Up yours," Dave replied. "Where's my glass?"

"You know you don't use a glass."

"I expect to be offered one anyway."

"Would you like a glass, Mister Garland?"

"No, thank you, John."

"Then up yours, Mister Garland." Murphy took a dollar bill from the bar, brought it to the register, and brought back a quarter change. "Thanks for the plug, by the way."

"Got to take care of my people."

"Next time you might mention that the fellow who owns the joint is a suave, deb-a-nare Irishman whom girls find irresistible."

"I'll try to remember."

"Bartender?"

They both looked up. The voice came from the other end of the bar. It belonged to a tall, leggy brunette with short hair and an interestingly pretty—as opposed to vacuously pretty—face.

She was about twenty-seven. She sat near the telephone, in front of the Big Ten roulette wheel which Johnny Murphy had picked up somewhere or other. She wore brown leather boots that came to mid-calf, a matching leather miniskirt that stopped just short of her panties, and a mannish white blouse with three buttons at the neck, all of them open. Under the blouse she seemed to be wearing no bra—unless it was one of those sheer keep-'em-from-flopping-but-don't-hide-the-natural-contours numbers.

Around her neck were several chains, from one of which hung a small, black Iron Cross. There was a plain, gold, three-decker ring on the fourth finger of her right hand, but nothing on the fourth finger of her left. She appeared to be admiringly aware of Dave Garland.

"Who is she?" he asked, *sotto voce.*

Johnny Murphy shrugged. "Never saw her before tonight. She came in about eleven." He smiled at her. "Another champagne cocktail, dear?"

"Please." She smiled back sweetly.

He dropped some ice into a cocktail shaker. Dave gazed at the girl. It was his interested-if-you-are-but-don't-let-it-go-to-your-head-because-I-can-survive-without-you number. She turned away.

"Not bad," he told Murphy.

"Forget it. She's waiting for somebody."

"At one thirty ayem?"

"So she says." He shrugged. "And I believe it. Guys've been striking out all night."

Dave swigged his beer. "Maybe I'll break the losing streak." Deliberately not looking at her, he held up an index finger to Murphy and said at double his previous volume, "One game, Murph?"

"Cry Bastion?" Murphy replied, picking up the cue. His natural acting talents rose to the surface as he did an exaggerated, eyes-widened take, reminiscent of Jerry Colonna. "You're a glutton for punishment, Dave."

"Shut up and set up the board."

Murphy produced a lidless cigar box from under the bar. It contained eight whiskey corks and eight champagne corks. He put the box in front of Dave, then finished mixing the champagne cocktail and brought it to the girl.

When he came back, Dave had arranged the corks on the bar in four lines of four, facing each other, like checkers.

"Move," said Murphy.

Dave moved a piece vaguely in the direction of his host's two rows.

Murphy promptly moved a rear-row piece to one side.

Dave moved another piece forward.

Murphy moved another to one side.

The two men's faces twisted in apparent concentration as three more moves were made—none of them suggesting any pattern or purpose. Then Dave suddenly moved two pieces to bracket one of Murphy's and cried, "Palfrey's gambit!"

"You dirty dog."

The girl at the other end of the bar did not conceal her interest. Absently sipping her champagne cocktail, she moved a seat closer.

Murphy watched her through the corner of his eye. "Are we playing Copenhagen rules?"

"Suit yourself."

Murphy reached tentatively for one of his corks.

"Careful."

The girl, obviously intrigued, moved another seat closer.

"Cry Bastion!" Murphy called, suddenly making a move.

"Sorry. No Bastion." Dave took one of Murphy's pieces.

"I didn't see that."

"Tough."

The girl moved another seat closer and watched Murphy take one of Dave's corks, then Dave take two of Murphy's.

"Very nice."

"Thank you."

"Here comes Copenhagen."

"Cry Bastion."

"No Bastion."

"Doggone! . . . Now Bastion."

"Bastion it is. Well done."

"And another!"

"Beautiful."

"Now—" Murphy beamed triumphantly as he reached for his forwardmost piece.

"Watch out, Murph."

The girl drained her drink, then left her stool and crossed to where Dave was sitting. He smiled at her as she peered intently over his shoulder. "He doesn't see it," he said, gesturing toward Murphy.

Murphy hesitated, then moved his cork. "Cry Bastion!"

"Fool's ploy!" Dave seized the cork, two others that flanked it, and one of his own. "Nice try, Murph, but you were outclassed." He turned to the girl. "You want to play the winner?"

"I'll just watch."

He patted the stool next to him. She sat as Dave and Murphy set up the corks again, then made a few moves.

"I'm Dave Garland," he said.

"I'm Evelyn Draper."

"Like a drink?"

"Okay."

"Nice game," said Murphy, picking up the corks and putting them back into the cigar box.

Evelyn Draper did a double-take. "What happened?"

"I won."

"How? When?"

"When you said okay," Murphy chuckled, retreating to the other end of the bar.

Evelyn looked evenly at Dave. "I ought to be mad."

"But you're not."

She smiled. "Not really."

THREE

She had been as easy to pick up as a dose of gonorrhea, Dave reflected as they rode in his MG to her apartment.

He immediately castigated himself for his choice of simile.

Don't put the chick down, Garland. She digs you. Is that such a crime? You never used to knock a chick for responding to your charm—not in the old days. Has Tobie got you turned inside out?

Well, of course, Tobie had him turned inside out. That much was conceded.

Still, there was something funny about the way this chick—this Evelyn Draper—responded to him. Not the slightest resistance. Or hesitation. Or apparent qualm.

It was as if she had been waiting there in the bar just for him.

Have a drink?

Why thank you very much.

Nice night, blah-blah-blah.

Lovely, isn't it?

Live around here?

Not too far, blah-blah-blah.

Another drink?

Don't mind if I do.

Blah-blah-blah.

Blah-blah-blah.

Yawn.

Tired?

Afraid so. Long day, blah-blah-blah.

Ride home?

Why, thank you very much. . . .

It was too pat—like Cry Bastion.

"I don't think I've been stood up on a date since I was in the ninth grade back in North Platte," she was saying.

He glanced at her in the dashboard mirror. There was, he decided, something very familiar about her. But he couldn't figure out what.

"Something wrong?" Her eyes met his in the mirror.

He realized he had been frowning. "No." He returned his gaze to the road. "I just keep thinking I know you from somewhere."

"I'll bet you say that to all the girls."

"No, seriously—"

"Hey! This is my exit!"

He wedged the MG between a Volkswagen and a Mercedes in the middle lane, then swung into the right lane just in time to navigate the exit ramp. She directed him along the access road, then through a maze of irregular blocks to a small apartment building that was identical to the dozens that stretched out on both sides of it.

"Well," she said as he halted at the curb, "thanks very much for the drinks and the ride, Mister—uh, Garland, is it?"

"Garland it is."

"Come in for a nightcap?"

He hesitated. Then he silently berated himself for hesitating.

Imagine feeling guilty about being unfaithful to a chick that walked out on you four months ago!

Besides, he reminded himself, he wanted to find out why this new chick seemed so familiar to him.

Oh, hey, fella! Now that's going *too* far! Since when do you have to make excuses for following up on a chick who's obviously giving you the high-sign?

"Well?" She was smiling expectantly. "Nightcap?"

"Yeah," he said. "Why not?"

Her apartment was the usual working-girl's living room, sleeping alcove, and kitchen. "Light a fire for me?" she asked, gesturing as she retreated to the kitchen.

The combustibles were prepared as if in anticipation of a visit: a thin layer of newspapers, then kindling, then logs. All he had to do was apply the flame.

He took a cigarette lighter from his pocket, flicked it open, then stared vacantly at the inscription on the case:

To Dave Garland, always the greatest. Love, Tobie.

"There are some matches in the orange vase," Evelyn Draper called from the kitchen.

Dave continued to stare at the lighter. He remembered the night Tobie had given it to him. His thirty-second birthday. He had been in the dumps about growing older—halfway between birth and social security, closer to age forty than age twenty-one, fourteen years past his mental prime, eight years past his physical.

"Look at the bright side," she had said. "Three years from now you'll be old enough to run for President."

Tobie, Tobie, please come back. I never realized how much I need you.

"Did you find them?" Evelyn called from the kitchen.

Dave went to the door. "Uh, honey—" Sheepish smile. Smile that says more than words can say. "It's getting late. Maybe I oughtta—"

She looked up from the ice cube tray that she was prying at with a butcher knife. Her eyes held his and, for a moment, her face was expressionless. Then, slowly, she returned his smile—but with a satisfied self-confidence that he found disconcerting.

"Dave—" She started toward him. "I didn't have a date tonight. I went to the Sardine Factory because you talk about it all the time on your program, and I just wanted to meet you." She stood in front of him, waiting for him to take her in his arms. "I listen to you all the time."

He turned away awkwardly. "I knew there was somebody out there," he managed to murmur.

"You're making fun of me."

"No I'm not. I'm just—" He turned to her again and now, suddenly, his eyes became animated. "Hey—say something else."

"Such as?"

"Such as asking me to light a fire for you."

Her brow furrowed. "Light a fire for me?" she finally said with exactly the same inflection as before.

He grinned. "Now, ask me to play *Misty* for you."

"Very good." She smiled. Then her smile faded as, once having identified her, he seemed to lose interest. She stared at the fireplace. "You didn't light the fire, Dave."

"Maybe I'd better take off."

"Don't you like me?"

"You're a very nice girl."

"But who needs nice girls?"

"I like nice girls." He weighed the cigarette lighter in his hand. "Problem is, I happen to be hung up on one."

"And you don't want to complicate your life?"

"That's about it." He suddenly was finding it hard to breathe. He had a mad impulse to run from the room.

"I don't want to complicate my life, either."

She went to the fireplace, found a long wooden match, struck it, and touched it several times to the underlayer of newspaper. As the flames rose she turned to Dave and smiled with something resembling little-girl innocence. "But that's no reason why we shouldn't sleep together if we feel like it."

He cocked a quizzical eyebrow at her.

Her smile broadened ever so slightly and her eyes suddenly were sparkling with invitation. "Well?"

The fire started to blaze as she stepped into his arms. He thrust his tongue deep into her mouth and knew that, for tonight at least, the pain of being without Tobie Williams wouldn't be quite so intense.

FOUR

"Well, well, talk about style!" Al Monte grinned as he burst into the living room. "This, dear fans, is how your idol lives—black kimono, bottle of beer, the Trane on the stereo . . . who could ask for anything more?"

Dave Garland looked up from his typewriter. "Didn't anybody ever tell you it's polite to knock?"

"You disc jockeys lead such exciting lives. Small wonder girls can't wait to get their hands on you."

"Yeah. We've got to beat 'em off with a club. Now, speaking of beating off—"

Al stretched out in the amoeba-shaped lounge chair next to the typewriter. "I've got a better idea. In case your tummy hasn't sent the message up to brainy-boy, it's dinner time. What say we pay a visit to my new sponsor, Mama Rios? It's a new Mexican place in Carmel and the albondigas soup is not to be believed.

A total mind blower. Kids are fixing with it." He pantomimed a hypodermic injection. "Right into the vein."

"Sorry, Al. I've got too much work to do."

"You've got to eat."

"I'll fix something here."

Al picked up the bottle of beer, held it up to the light, frowned disapprovingly, then drank it. "I'm beginning to worry about your social life, friend. To say nothing of your health, if you continue to drink rotgut like this."

"You'll make somebody a fine mother."

"Never. Too narrow in the pelvis."

"Too narrow in the head, you mean." Dave started for the door. "Seriously, babes, I'm working up a presentation for the Frisco gig. Be a pal and get lost, okay?"

"Never let it be said that Al Monte can't take a hint." He stepped ceremonially to one side of the door, which Dave promptly opened with a flourish.

Standing on the doorstep was Evelyn Draper, her arms full of grocery bags which she was having a hard time juggling as she tried to ring the bell with her elbow. Somehow her splendid, uncorsetted breasts managed to obtrude amidst the bags.

"Hi," she said, "I was just in the neighborhood and—" She seemed suddenly to notice that Al wasn't the person she had come to see. Smiling tentatively she said, "Is this where Dave Garland lives?"

"If you call it living." Al ushered her inside. His

eyes scanned her body appreciatively. "And I, for one, very definitely call it living."

She brushed past him and noticed Dave. "Hi," she beamed with airline stewardess cheeriness. "Thought you might like a bite to eat." She looked for the kitchen door, found it and vanished inside with her packages. "Excuse me," she called over her shoulder, "but these things weigh a ton."

Al winked broadly as he watched her shapely calves disappear through the doorway. "I know, I know, she's from Chicken Delight." He half-skipped, half-slid toward the outside door with a burlesque comic's gait, then made a that's-all-folks gesture with an imaginary straw hat. "Don't work too hard on that Frisco presentation, buddy-boy." He ducked outside, letting the door slam.

Dave went to the kitchen. A scowl was trying to take possession of his face and he offered only token resistance. He was angry. Evelyn Draper wasn't playing by the rules.

"Evelyn," he said, "you and I have got to have a little talk."

"What's this, a shrunken head?" she asked, kneeling in front of the refrigerator. She held up a shriveled radish by its top leaf. Other than beer it was the only thing in the box. Almost as an afterthought and with a touch of possessiveness, she asked, "Who's that guy? Your roommate?"

Dave's scowl deepened. "Come here, Evelyn."

She turned back to the refrigerator, putting things away, talking too fast. "Can't leave this stuff out too long. Let's see, now: I hope you like porterhouse steak. You look like a steak-and-potatoes type. And–"

"Listen, Evelyn–"

"–I thought a green salad with tomatoes and a nice Roquefort–"

"Whoa! Not another word!" He held up his hand. "Your solicitude and generosity, young lady, are appreciated. But there's a house rule here against uninvited guests."

Instantly she stopped chattering and turned to him, her expression contrite, almost pleading. "Don't send me away, David. Please." She looked up at him with unwavering, almost childlike eyes.

He felt his anger starting to ebb and made an effort to hold on to it. Give in now, Garland, and she'll feel free to come and go as she pleases.

"I just wanted to surprise you, David. I thought you might be hungry, and–"

"And what if Al and I had been talking business? Or if I'd had a chick up here–and in you come with an armload of groceries!"

She lowered her eyes, even more childlike than before. "I'm sorry, David." She slowly got to her feet and started toward the living room. "You might as well keep those," she said, gesturing toward the groceries. "I seem to have lost my appetite." She moved quickly past him toward the door.

Almost in spite of himself, he reached out and caught her arm. "Wait a minute."

She averted her gaze.

"Look at me, Evelyn." He took her face between

his hands and slowly turned her head so that she could not avoid looking directly into his eyes. "I'm trying to tell you something, baby. Don't push me too hard, dig? It makes for a sticky situation and sticky situations make me want to run."

"I don't understand, David. Should I go? Should I stay? What do you want me to do?"

"I want you to realize that there's such a thing as a telephone. I dial it, and you say hello, and I say what are you doing?"

She grinned. "And I say I'll be right over."

"Next time, let's try it that way."

"Okay." Her grin broadened and took on a faintly triumphant glimmer. It was the "next time" that did it. "How do you like your porterhouse?" she asked, beginning to unpack the rest of the groceries.

"Extremely rare," he murmured, retreating to the living room.

He hated himself for giving in to her so quickly, and hated himself even more for letting his sexual longings get the better of his judgment. But it had been a long time between drinks. And, as Al Monte might put it, a bird in the hand is no substitute for a bird in the nest.

Dave selected a bottle from the walnut wine rack next to the fireplace, poured two glasses of Beaujolais and sat on the couch contemplating his while he listened to Evelyn clatter about in the kitchen.

Don't be so defensive, he told himself. There's nothing to be uptight about. The chick heard your voice, dug your rap and decided to do a number with you. It's been known to happen.

So don't be a jerk. Take what she has to offer and be glad she's offering it. Use her and then, when you get tired of her, give her the gate. What's the big deal?

There was, of course, no big deal. But he seemed unable to resist making it a big deal.

"Whatever happened to that bit about no strings?" he asked as she came out of the living room to claim her wine and announce that the steaks would be ready in a jif.

"No strings?" Her eyebrows arched quizzically. Then she chuckled softly, came over to him, and stood very close. "There are no strings, David. But I never said anything about not coming back for seconds, did I?"

Her breasts grazed his belly and the familiar stirrings of passion suddenly welled up inside him. She pressed closer and noticed his arousal. "Shall I turn off the steak?"

His only reply was to kiss her, hard.

"I'll turn off the steak," she said. She scampered into the kitchen and returned almost instantly, grinning like a mischievous child. "You know, David, you're a very sexy man."

He scooped her up and carried her to the bedroom.

"A very sexy man," she repeated as he lowered himself on top of her. "Can't even wait till after din-din."

He started to say something, then changed his mind. All of a sudden he was in no mood for conversation. A very sexy man, she had said. Perhaps a very horny man would be more accurate.

He made love to her passionately, almost desperately, as if he were trying to lose himself in her leggy loveliness. When it was over he held her close, glad—even grateful—that she had barged into his life. Maybe, he told himself, she was just what he needed right now.

They lay together silently for a while, then made love again. Then she got up, washed and served dinner.

The steaks were just right. They ate them—and the salad with the Roquefort dressing—sitting cross-legged in front of the fireplace. Then they finished the bottle of Beaujolais and made love again. This time he didn't even bother to carry her to the bedroom.

Drowsy from wine and lovemaking, he dozed off. He was awakened by the first streaks of light pouring through the window. He peered at his watch. Four fifty-two.

He yawned, stretched and yawned again. Then he gently prodded Evelyn. "Time for you to go home," he said as she opened her eyes.

Obediently, she rose and dressed. He escorted her to the driveway where a two-year-old, cream-colored Ford that looked as though it was falling apart was parked behind his MG. She slid behind the wheel.

"Well, good night," he said. "Or good morning. Or whatever." He yawned.

"When will I see you?" she asked, switching on the ignition.

"I'll give you a ring."

Her engine sputtered to life. She offered Dave a sexy laugh. "David, did anyone ever tell you you're a very funny man?"

"How's that?" he asked sleepily.

"Oh, well, if you want to keep playing the little games, we'll play them. But really, darling, it isn't necessary any more. At least not for me."

He looked at her, puzzled. He started to ask what she meant, but was interrupted by a deep masculine "Hey!"

A head was protruding from the window of the house next door. It belonged to a man named Tom Miller. "People trying to sleep here," he called grumpily.

"People trying to talk here," Evelyn retorted.

"Hey, smart-ass—how'd you like it if I called the cops?"

"Hey, hard-ass—how'd you like to go screw yourself?" Evelyn Draper's smile grew wicked. She rammed the heel of her hand down on the horn.

For a split-second Dave could only stare at her, utterly flabbergasted. Then he reached through the window and pried her hand free. "Cool it. The man's only asking to sleep."

Her eyes had a strange, wild look, almost as if she didn't recognize him. Then, with snap-of-the-finger suddenness, they cleared and she smiled radiantly. "It's such a lovely morning. Why be selfish with it?"

Tom Miller slammed his window shut in final protest. Evelyn put the Ford in gear, blew Dave a kiss and drove away.

FIVE

Let me go-o,
Let me go-o,
Let me go,
Lover. . . .

Tobie Williams wouldn't let him go. The two nights with Evelyn Draper should have exorcised her memory, or at least diminished her impact upon him. But a few hours after he and Evelyn had parted, the memory would come back full-strength and he would almost ache to be with her.

The problem, Dave theorized, was that Evelyn was too wild, too off-the-wall. She was one of those chicks that you balled because she was groovy, but that you could never get serious about because something warned you there'd be nothing but headaches ahead.

No, that wasn't the problem. At least, it wasn't the main problem. The main problem was that Dave was hopelessly in love with Tobie Williams.

The first month after she'd left hadn't been too bad. He had been more surprised and annoyed by her disappearance than pained by it and he had been confident that she'd be back before long. When he thought about her, it was usually in connection with how he planned to chew her out for vanishing without letting him know where she was going and when she'd be back.

Then the second month passed and there still was no trace of her. He had contacted everyone who might know her whereabouts and had drawn nothing but blanks. His annoyance turned then to hurt and loss. He knew that nothing had happened to her because every week or so that faggot agent of hers, Jay-Jay, displayed a new piece of her sculpture in his gallery. But Jay-Jay wouldn't say where she was and neither would anyone else.

Now she had been gone four months and there still was no trace of her. Each day made him more painfully aware of her absence.

Just one more chance,
To prove that you're the one I care for,
Each night I say a little prayer for . . .

Shit!

He wheeled the MG around a corner, pulled to a

halt in the bumper-to-bumper downtown traffic and casually scanned the crowd on the sidewalk.

He was, he realized, searching for her—though he knew she wouldn't be there. He searched all the time lately. And every so often, when he'd spot a wind-blown head of straw-blonde hair, his pulse would quicken—even though he was sure the girl wasn't she.

Ridiculous?

Of course it was ridiculous. And that was what made the whole thing so frustrating.

The traffic inched ahead and he inched the MG along with it. As he scanned the crowd farther down the block, his breath suddenly caught in his lungs and his heart began pounding so loud he was sure she could hear it.

The girl he spotted was too far away to be seen clearly and her hair was black instead of straw-blonde. But there was no mistaking the loud, orange-and-white-striped fisherman's sweater she was wearing. It was the one Tobie had knitted for herself last fall. There couldn't be another like it on the whole Monterey Peninsula.

"Tobie!" he shouted, standing up in the car. "Hey, Tobie!"

The girl in the fisherman's sweater kept walking away from him.

He tromped on the emergency brake, jumped out of the car and, leaving it in the middle of the street, chased after her.

"Hey!" he called as she disappeared around the corner.

He broke into a full-speed run and rounded the corner just in time to catch sight of her vanishing into a boutique. When he got to the boutique, she was standing at a counter examining Mexican shawls.

"Hey!" he said, coming up behind her.

"Yes?" She turned.

He stared, stunned. She was slim and dark with a dancer's body and the face of an Aztec princess. She was beautiful. But she was not Tobie Williams.

"My mistake," he muttered. "That sweater—I thought you were somebody else. Excuse me." He started back to the street.

"Wait. You must be David."

He turned slowly to face her. "Who are you?"

"Anjelica. Tobie's new roommate."

"Where is she?"

Anjelica consulted her watch. "By now she should be at the gallery."

Dave didn't waste time with amenities. Murmuring a quick "nice to have met you," he trotted back to the car—which was tying up traffic for blocks—and sped to the ornate two-story converted frame house on the outskirts of the city identified to passersby by an antique physician's shingle reading CHEZ JAY-JAY.

Dave went to the back door, which opened into the gallery workshop. A bell tinkled sharply as he entered.

A petite blonde in her early twenties sat at a table in the center of the shop. She wore a pale blue, man's workshirt, a leather thong necklace and welder's goggles. In her hand was an acetylene torch; she was focusing its flame on a small copper figure.

She looked up when she heard the bell, stared blankly at Dave for a moment, then slowly pushed the goggles onto her head and smiled. "Hi. Long time no see."

"Where the hell have you been?" he demanded, glowering despite his resolution to be all sweetness and light.

"Here and there." When his only reaction was to tighten his clenched jaws, she added, "I was trying to join the contemporary revolt against the representational and not quite making it." She smiled wryly. "And now I'm trying to act flip and aloof and cool and I'm not quite making that either. Sorry, Dave."

His expression softened. He came to her side and put his hand on her shoulder. "When did you get back?"

"Night before last. I was going to phone you."

"But you couldn't find a dime?"

"I really was, Dave. Don't be sarcastic, please. I just needed a little more time. To get settled."

"I'm sorry. About the sarcasm." He stroked her neck. "I missed you."

"I missed you, too. Though I promised myself I'd never admit it." She pressed her cheek against his chest. "You've gotten thinner."

"And you've gotten fatter," came a high-pitched, effeminate squeal from the far side of the room. "Right between the ears!"

Dave glanced up at a tall, stocky, gray-haired man who glided across the workshop as smoothly as if he were riding a miniature unicycle. He wore a pale gray one-piece knit jumpsuit with a gleaming silver zipper in front and a heavy silver chain-belt draped over his abundant hips. His eyelashes were subtly darkened with mascara and he held one arm cocked just below his chest with the wrist so limp that the muscles supporting it might have been cut.

"Hi, Jay-Jay," Dave said. "Still your old charming self, I see."

The owner of Chez Jay-Jay glided past without acknowledging him. "So much for Sausalito," he hissed, viper-like, at Tobie.

"Sausalito?" Dave echoed.

"That's where I was staying. At Jay-Jay's place."

Dave shot the gallery owner an annoyed look. "Your place?"

"Nothing much, really. Just a little *pied-à-terre*. But it's handy to the fleet."

"You told me you didn't know where she was."

"So I lied. Sue me." He took a satin handkerchief from his pocket and dabbed at a nearby piece of sculpture, as if dusting it. "Besides, it wasn't my idea. You should have caught her act before she left. The whole Bette Davis 'through-finished-kaput' scene. At three ayem, yet."

"Oh, come on, Jay-Jay," said Tobie. Glancing at Dave, she added, "He's exaggerating."

Jay-Jay favored her with an I-think-you're-out-of-your-mind-but-it's-your-funeral look. "What happened, pussycat? Did you weaken and give him a call?"

"He ran into Anjelica. She told him I was here."

"For which she should be hanged by the thumbs, or some equally appropriate appendage." He spun away, as if metaphorically to reinforce his dissociation from their reunion and glided over to a color field painting on a distant wall. He painstakingly righted the angle at which it hung.

Swiftly Dave reached over, plucked the torch from Tobie's hand and flicked off the flame. Then he removed the goggles from atop her head and handed them to her. "Let's go," he said.

She hesitated briefly, then started toward the closet. "I'll get my jacket."

"Oh, joy!" sighed Jay-Jay. "Just two minutes of exposure to him and four months of resolution crumble." Turning to Dave, he added, "Nothing personal, mind you. I just think she could be a first-rate artist if her hormones didn't keep getting in the way."

"Jay-Jay," Dave replied, heading for the door as Tobie reappeared with the jacket over her arm, "why don't you go cruise for some sailors?"

"Please," said the gallery owner, exaggerating an expression of disgust as he held up one hand in a gesture of protest, "Gastronomically, it's been a very difficult week. Don't mention seafood."

Outside, Dave held the car door open for Tobie, then went around to his own side and started the engine. As he revved it up, he gently covered her hand with his. Slowly she drew away.

He looked to her for an explanation.

"I'm sorry," she said softly. "I realize I might have given you the impression in there that I wanted to touch you again, but what Jay-Jay said brought me to my senses. I did resolve to call it quits, Dave. I think it'll be better for both of us if we do."

"Why?"

"I—" She paused, then glanced back at the door to the gallery. "Could we drive to the beach?"

"Sure." He quickly navigated the dozen blocks leading to the access road to the coastal highway. As he pulled into the stream of traffic, he glanced at her in the rearview mirror.

She stared straight ahead and said nothing.

"Well?" he prodded. "Why?"

"On the beach, David. Please don't rush me."

He drove the rest of the way in silence. Finally, when they were alone on the sand, she said, "I really missed the beach. I even dreamed about it sometimes."

"I missed you. I dreamed about you all the time."

"You'd be doing me a terrific favor if you didn't say things like that."

"Why?"

"It brings out the worst in me. It makes me want to say things like, 'How's the redhead?' "

"What redhead?"

"You know. From the bookstore. She walked with a kind of wiggle."

"Oh, that redhead." He laughed. "She went back to Berkeley—or wherever."

"Too bad. But you always had that blonde from Santa Barbara to fall back on, if that's the phrase I'm looking for. And I think it is."

He stared out at the ocean and felt his stomach tightening into a knot. "Is that what we're going to do? Go down the list?"

"Who's got that kind of time?" She started away from the shoreline, toward a densely foliated, lushly green woodland a hundred yards inland.

For a long moment he stood where he was, silently staring after her. Then he broke into a jog and drew up alongside her. "Look, I'm sorry about the other girls. All of them. Isn't there some way you can give me blanket absolution for the whole lot?"

"You've got me mixed up with the Catholic Church."

"No. You're prettier." He gently touched her face. "And softer."

"And faster on my feet." She laughed, dashing away from him. He chased her through the woodland and into the tall sea grass on the other side. She managed a few dozen yards in the grass, then lost her footing and fell breathlessly to the ground.

He dropped to his knees alongside her and again reached for her face.

"No, Dave." She turned away. "Please don't."

"But for Pete's sake, Tobie, why? I don't get it."

She got to her feet and started walking again. "For one thing, I'm chicken. And for another, it's just dumb. After all those days and nights watching the sun come up and go down, just thinking about what was wrong with us and why we had to end it—and now to come back and, bang, start right in exactly where we left off —it's . . ." She broke off and shook her head in exasperation.

"Well," he said impatiently, "where exactly would you like to start in?"

She stared at the sand. "I just don't think I'm up to it any more, Dave. Those nights sitting home waiting for you to finish your show and come by. And then it would start getting late, and I'd say to myself, well he's either run his car over a cliff or he's run into a blonde. Then one night I found I was really kind of rooting for the accident." She smiled ruefully. "I mean, if it had to be that or the blonde."

"I can't tell you how touched I am."

"I didn't wish you anything really serious."

"That's considerate of you."

"Just a couple of months in traction."

"You're all heart."

She stopped abruptly on a dune and stood looking out at the ocean. The wind whipped her blonde hair around her face, making her look very young and fragile. "If there's anything I hate," she said, "it's a jealous female. And that's exactly what I was turning into." She wrinkled her nose in distaste. "That's why I had to bail out, Dave. I was getting to be one of my own unfavorite people."

He started to reach again for her face, but restrained himself. "You know, Tobe, ever since you left there's been a little empty space in my life that's just about your size. I've learned my lesson."

"Lots of girls my size—if you're really looking."

"I'm not. That's what I'm trying to say."

She turned away from him and resumed walking. He followed.

Without looking up, she asked, "You don't expect me to believe you've given up girls, do you?"

"I'm ready to—if you're ready to start all over with me."

"Better not do it too suddenly. We don't want the groupies to riot."

"Now, wait a minute, Tobe." He grabbed her hand and roughly turned her around. "You're not being fair. It wasn't all my fault, remember."

"Oh? They overpowered you, is that it?"

"You've got a little piece of the blame, too, you know. You and that parade of roomies that kept moving in and out of your place. There we were—you and me in front of the fireplace and across the room some chick sitting there in a wool bathrobe eating fig newtons."

"We've been through this before, Dave. When my father left me the house, he also left me the monthly payments. I just can't handle all the expenses alone. And don't remind me about your offer to pay half of them, because I'm not going to accept money from anyone I'm not married to—" She choked off the sentence. "That's neither a threat nor a proposal, by the way. Just a simple statement of fact."

"Then here's another one. I want to marry you."

She looked at him disbelievingly for a long moment. Then slowly she shook her head. "Not under these circumstances, Dave. Not if I feel that I coerced you into it."

"Well, for Pete's sake! You don't want to get married, you don't want to move in with me, you don't want to take up where we left off—what *do* you want?"

Softly she said, "A little time, Dave. A week or two more, to get my head together."

"Fair enough." He reached again for her face.

She again turned away. "Not until I've made up my mind, Dave. I don't think I could handle it if I let my hormones get in the way, as Jay-Jay would put it." She started in the direction from which they had come. "Will you give me a ride home now?"

"Yeah." He followed her toward the highway.

"Please understand that it has to be this way," she said as they rode toward her house. "I have to make the decision for myself. I'll let you know when I've made it."

"In other words, it's 'Don't call me, I'll call you'?"

"I'm sorry, Dave, but I'm afraid that's what it is."

They rode the rest of the way to her house in silence. "Thanks," she said as he pulled into the driveway. "I will call, Dave. Either way. I promise."

"Hey, there you are!" squealed a high-pitched voice from up on the porch. Anjelica came bounding toward the car. "I see you found each other."

"Yeah." Dave swallowed hard.

"Would you like to come in for some coffee?" Tobie asked, almost as an afterthought.

"With fig newtons?" He scowled. "I'll wait for your

call." He pulled out of the driveway and sped toward the coastal highway.

What he would do, he decided, was go home and take a good hot shower, get to the station early for a change, do his show, then go to the Sardine Factory and throw the drunk to end all drunks.

Then he remembered that today was his day off. He decided to go straight to the Sardine Factory and get an early start.

SIX

The phone was ringing as Dave walked into the bar. Johnny Murphy made an it's-for-you gesture as he answered it.

"Who?" Dave mouthed silently.

"You say this is Evelyn?" Murphy said into the phone.

Dave shook his head as he went behind the bar and helped himself to a beer.

"You just missed him," said Murphy. He paused a moment, then added, "Seriously, honey, he left about ten minutes ago. Now, if you're interested in someone a little more on the suave, distinguished side—mustache, big brown eyes, snazzy dresser—I'll be happy to . . ." He winced, stared disbelievingly at the receiver for a moment, then replaced it in its cradle. "That chick has a very dirty mouth." He crossed behind the bar to the bulletin board. "By the way, you're very popular today. Some other broad called from San Francisco. Madge somebody."

"Brenner?"

"Yeah." Murphy took a thumbtacked note off the bulletin board and handed it to Dave. "Your pal Monte gave her this number."

Dave read the note: "Your foto and biography rec'd. My people very interested. Imperative you send two-hour tape of your show immediately."

"Well," he said, draining his beer, "there go my plans for the drunk to end all drunks."

Outside, he noticed that the front door of the MG was ajar. He was positive he hadn't left it that way. He went to the car; Evelyn Draper was there, hunched all the way down on the floor of the front seat.

"Surprise," she said, smiling brightly as she looked up at him.

He frowned. "What are you doing here?"

"Waiting for you, of course." She straightened up in the seat and gestured to a phone booth across the street. "I called the Sardine Factory from there. It was funny—Murphy telling me you left ten minutes ago, and me standing outside watching through the window while you drank your beer." She widened her eyes in the innocent-little-girl look he was coming to know very well—and despise. "Don't you think that's funny?"

"Hilarious," he murmured, putting his keys in the ignition.

"You know, David, when you lie you should be

careful that the person you're lying to can't catch you in the act."

"Evelyn," he said through tightened jaws, "let me enlighten you on a couple of matters: number one, I don't dig playing spy games; number two, when I want to talk to a girl on the phone, I call her, she doesn't call me. Understand?"

She laughed. "You know, David, your nostrils flare out like little wings when you're mad. It's kind of cute."

"The point is, beat it."

"I'd love a drink, David."

"Some other time. I've got to get to the station."

"You're talking to your number one fan, darling. Tonight's your night off."

"I don't feel I owe you an explanation, but, for the record, I've got a show to set."

"What do you mean, 'set'?"

"Put together. Pick the music, write the lead-ins, choose the poetry."

"I'll help you. I know all kinds of poetry. By heart."

"No, Evelyn. I don't need help. And I don't want help. And if I ever do want your help, I'll ask for it. Now, please get out of the car, because I'd like to leave."

"Well, talk about gratitude!" Her voice rose shrilly. "Here I give you everything I have, hold nothing back and that's the thanks I get—"

"Now wait a minute, baby! Don't go doing that sacrifice number on me. You've done nothing you didn't want to do—"

She lunged at him as if she were going to strike him. He raised his arms in defense. She quickly ducked beneath them, then just as quickly darted away.

The maneuver mystified him until he recognized what she was dangling tauntingly before his eyes as she leaned back against the door: the keys she had just swiped from his ignition.

"Give them back, Evelyn." He held out his hand, palm up.

She giggled mischievously, then opened the door and skipped nimbly out of the car. "Does he want his keys?" she baby-talked, holding them high in the air.

"Come on," he said, his anger growing.

She backed away, still holding the keys up tauntingly. "Speak, doggie. Say bow-wow."

He stared, enraged and incredulous. "What are you trying to prove?"

She backed farther away, dangling the keys enticingly. "Nice doggie. Don't be mad. Say bow-wow for Evelyn."

He bounded out of the car after her as she ran toward the nearest building, a garage with an outdoor stairway leading to a second-story cocktail lounge. She trotted up the stairway with him close behind.

She stopped at the top and looked down at him, her expression a mixture of excitement, defiance and amusement. He was about five steps beneath her now. He stopped and, with an effort, kept his temper under control.

"All right, Evelyn," he said through gritted teeth, "give me the keys."

She smiled saccharinely and gestured toward the door of the cocktail lounge. "You might as well buy me a drink as long as we're here."

"Just give me the keys, Evelyn."

Smiling more broadly, she raised her hand as though she were going to toss the keys down into the street. He swiftly bounded up the remaining stairs, seized her wrist and forced the keys loose.

"You son of a bitch," she hissed as he caught them. She swung at him with her free arm.

As if on cue, the door of the cocktail lounge opened and two men in business suits came out. "Having trouble, Miss?" asked one.

"Beat it," Dave snarled, still holding her at bay.

The two men hesitated, torn between the desire to help a pretty girl in distress and the wish to avoid an ugly encounter. The younger and heavier man looked at Evelyn. "Well, Miss?"

"You heard the gentleman," she snapped. "Get lost—asshole."

The two men exchanged bewildered looks, then moved past Evelyn and Dave down the steps into the street.

"I guess I told 'em, huh, pal?" she asked, laughing.

"Evelyn," he said softly, holding the keys tightly and beyond her reach, "I'm going to leave now. Please don't give me any more trouble."

She put on her innocent-little-girl look. "Trouble, David? Why on earth would I want to give you any trouble?"

He walked slowly down the stairs, half expecting

that at any moment she would leap upon him like some crazy woman out of an Alfred Hitchcock film, going for his jugular with an icepick. When he reached his car, he looked back and found her standing where he had left her.

"'Bye," she called, smiling sweetly as she waved. "See you later."

"No way," he murmured under his breath as he waved back . . . no possible way in the world, baby, because you are a looney bird if ever I have seen one and whenever I spot a looney bird my instinct is to cut out.

As a matter of fact, he told himself as he drove to the radio station, he should have cut out before this. When she showed up the day before yesterday with the porterhouse steaks, he should have unceremoniously given her the old heave-ho. He had gone through enough super-fans in the past to recognize a hold-tight chick when he saw one. Don't give 'em any encouragement and they won't give you any grief.

Oh, well, better late than never. She knew now where it was at and, if she showed up again, she'd get the same message in triplicate.

He wheeled the MG out of its parking place, around a corner and into the downtown traffic. It was getting windy and the air blowing through his hair felt good. If Madge Brenner and her people liked his show, it could be the start of a whole new life for him. And there was no reason why they shouldn't like the show.

What he would do, he mused, was take Tobie to San Francisco with him. Clean break with the past. No more groupies, no more kookies, no more anything that was associated with the old life. Henceforth, Mister and Missus G in their comfy old split level overlooking the bay.

Assuming, of course, that Tobie wanted it.

But that was a safe assumption. If she hadn't wanted it, the hassles they'd had would never have arisen. Right? Right!

He pulled into his designated parking stall in the KRML lot. Suddenly he was all fired up to work on the tape for Madge Brenner. He had a feeling that if he just sat down at the console and let himself go, he'd produce one of the finest shows he had ever done.

SEVEN

It was a great show. As he recorded it he realized it was first rate—the music perfectly matched to the talk, all the cues nice and tight, his inflections just right when he read. Listening to the playback reinforced the feeling. Madge Brenner and her people would flip; they'd have no choice.

He left the studio feeling better than he had in a long while. Now, if only Tobie would call—

He thought of stopping by the Sardine Factory, then decided against it. Crazy Evelyn might be there and he wasn't in the mood for another battle with her. Better go straight home and get a good night's sleep. With luck, Tobie might have made a quick decision and the message would be waiting for him with his answering service.

He grinned exultantly as he pulled the MG to a halt

in his driveway. Suddenly, everything seemed to be falling right for him. Tobie back, the Frisco gig as good as sewed up—who could ask for anything more?

He whistled *San Francisco, Open Your Golden Gate* as he strolled up his front walk. Then he stopped short as he saw the huge, stuffed animal propped against his door. It was a cerise velvet dog with floppy ears and a lolling tongue. Around its neck was a white satin ribbon with a note hanging from it.

Dave grinned again as he reached for the note. It was, he thought happily, from Tobie. It was just like her to choose this cute way of telling him that she had made up her mind.

He opened the note, and immediately his grin faded. The note read: "Hi. My name is Misty. Evelyn sent me to apologize to you. Please give her another chance."

He balled up the note and stuffed it into his pocket. Then he unlocked the door and was about to step inside when a female voice came out of the darkness alongside the stairs.

"Well," it asked, "is the apology accepted?"

"Evelyn," Dave sighed, "will you please get off my back?"

She stepped out from behind the small pine tree which she had been using as cover. Her gait was slightly wobbly, as if she had been drinking. "David, you're an awful host. The proper thing to say is, 'Hi, Evelyn, come in for a drink.' "

"No dice, Evelyn." He blocked the doorway. "Go home now, please, before you make me do something we'll both regret."

"There's only one thing you could do, David, that I'd regret and that's turn me away. Can't you see that all I want is to please you?"

"If you really want to please me, you'll leave me alone."

"You don't mean that, David. I realize you're trying to make things easy for that blonde bitch of yours. But don't you see, David, she doesn't really love you—I do."

He stared at her incredulously.

"You wonder how I know she's blonde, don't you?" She chuckled. "Well, I saw her picture on your dresser the last time we made love. Really, David, you should be more discreet about things like that. It's very unflattering to a girl to invite her into your bedroom to make love, then display a picture of another girl."

"Evelyn, I don't know quite how to put this tactfully, so I'll put it untactfully: you're becoming a king-sized pain in the ass. Will you please leave me alone?"

"David, David, David, don't you realize that we don't have to play these silly games any more?" She giggled weirdly. "Why are you pretending that you don't love me?"

"I *don't* love you, Evelyn. I never said I did."

"You didn't have to say it, David. You showed it. You showed it in millions of ways, even before we met. The way you used to answer the phone when I called to ask you to play *Misty* for me—" Her eyes took on a far-away look. "The way you looked at me that first night in the Sardine Factory—"

He listened with mounting disbelief as she continued to cite "evidence" of his love for her. Evelyn Draper wasn't merely a pain in the ass; she was a genuine nut.

But what to do with her?

"Evelyn," he said wearily, "I'm going inside now—alone. I think it would be a very good idea for you to go home and go to bed."

She grabbed his arm. "I'm going to stay here, David. If you won't take me in with you, I'm going to stand out here on the porch and embarrass you in front of all your neighbors." She looked at him challengingly for a moment; then, when he started into the house, she stepped back and shouted, "Hey, listen, everybody! I want to tell you all about Dave Garland. You've heard of the Big D? You've heard what a hot-shot he's supposed to be with women? Well, I've got news for you."

He struggled to cover her mouth. She broke away from him.

"Well," she continued, "he's a flop. A real washout. He can't get it up on a bet. And he's a liar. He tells girls he loves them, then—"

He finally managed to get his palm over her mouth, choking off her voice. "Evelyn, I'm not going to tolerate any more of this. In a minute I'm going to let you go. When I do, I want you to go quietly to your car and drive home and never bother me again. If you do, I swear I'll break your neck. Do you understand?"

She remained motionless. He waited for a moment, then released her—ready to clap his hand over her mouth again if she resumed her tirade.

"I'm half tempted to call your bluff," she said softly. "But I'll make a deal with you instead. Make love to me tonight—let me spend the night here with you—and I'll go away tomorrow morning and never bother you again."

If he believed her, he would have said yes. "No deals, Evelyn. It's all over. Period."

"I could make trouble for you, David. I could go to the police and say you tried to rape me. It'd be the end of your career. They always believe the girl, you know—"

"Good night, Evelyn." He started into the house.

"Wait, David!" She wedged her foot in the door.

"No, Evelyn. It's all over."

"Can I use your bathroom?"

He looked at her suspiciously.

"I have to go to the bathroom. Do you want me to go in my pants?"

He heaved a huge sigh. "All right, use the bathroom. But that's it—no fun and games afterward. Understand?"

"I promise you, David." She preceded him into the house. "There will be no fun and games afterward."

He stretched out on the couch and stared sightlessly at the ceiling as she locked herself inside the bathroom. Five minutes later, she still had not come out.

"Hey, Evelyn," he called, "you about ready?"

There was no answer.

He went to the door and listened intently. All he could hear was water trickling into the sink.

"Hey, Evelyn—come on, huh?"

No answer.

He tried the door. Still locked, of course.

"Evelyn, goddammit!—"

Still no answer—and now, suddenly, he could hear water splashing onto the floor. The sink evidently was overflowing.

"Evelyn, open the goddam door!" He shook the knob frantically, then braced himself to throw a shoulder into the door. Just then, he heard the latch being lifted.

The door swung open and Evelyn Draper stood framed in the doorway, her eyes puffy, her face streaked with mascara. "I'm your raven, Edgar Allan Garland," she said in a bizarre, far-away voice. "*Take thy beak from out my heart, take thy form from off my door! Quoth the Raven, 'Nevermore!'* Nevermore, David—do you understand me? Nevermore!"

She took a step toward him and held out her arms, wrists upward. His face went white and his knees buckled as he looked down at the blood-smeared gashes on each wrist.

EIGHT

Doctor Frank Dewan got to the apartment within five minutes of Dave's call. "Superficial," he pronounced after suturing the wounds. "She wasn't trying very hard, I'm afraid." He carried her into the bedroom, laid her out carefully on the bed and administered a hypodermic injection. "What do you do to evoke demonstrations like this, pal? I can't even get them to shed tears over me."

"The question is," Dave said dryly, "what do I do to get her *not* to favor me with a repeat performance?"

"Dial your local police department. There's a law in this state—difficult though it may seem to enforce—against suicide or any attempt thereat. The cops'll have her looked at by a psychiatrist and he'll put her away someplace nice and comfy, where she'll never bother you again."

"Yeah. Meanwhile all the papers have a field day with front page stories about the doll who tried to rub herself out in the apartment of the deejay who spurned her." He shook his head. "I can't afford it, Frank. Not with that Frisco gig hanging in the balance —to say nothing of my thing with Tobie."

The physician followed him into the kitchen, where Dave put on a pot of coffee. "I'm supposed to file a report even if you don't, Dave. I guess I can forget to file it. But judging from what you've told me about her, she's not the kind of chick that'll stop at this. She wants you, baby, and she'll use every trick in the book to get you."

Dave stared broodingly at the percolating coffee. "If only I could hold her off for a few weeks. Once the Frisco thing comes through and I get straight with Tobie, it'll be different." He looked hopefully at his friend. "Suppose I just stall her for a while? Do you think I could buy a couple of weeks' time without her doing something else violent?"

Frank Dewan shrugged. "One unfortunate thing about nutty broads, buddy, is that they're totally unpredictable. As for this one, I imagine she won't give you any trouble so long as she believes she's got you where she wants you. But let her start feeling rejected again, and there's no telling what she'll do."

"I suppose I could play games with her for a while —certainly until Tobie calls."

"And then?"

"I'll cross that bridge when I come to it."

They chatted about other things while they drank

their coffee. Finally, Frank looked at his watch. "I'm due in surgery a few hours from now, pal. Gotta get moving." At the door he said, "There'll be somebody around here today?"

"I'll be."

"Good. I bombed her out pretty good. She should wake up some time this afternoon and it'll help if there's somebody to play nursemaid for her. If I were you, I'd keep her here for two or three days and give her oodles of tender loving care."

"Oh, joy."

Frank laughed. "Now come on, pal—you can't say it'll be the most distasteful thing you've ever done. She's hardly what anybody would call a bad-looking chick."

"Yeah," Dave said, shaking hands goodbye, "it's just that she's in the wrong place at the wrong time."

He watched Frank drive off, then went to the kitchen and poured himself a cold beer. He was, he realized suddenly, physically and emotionally exhausted. He was too whipped even to finish the beer.

He drained the glass, then recapped the bottle and put it back in the refrigerator. He started for the bedroom, then changed his mind and went to the living room couch. He fell asleep almost instantly.

It was one in the afternoon when he awoke. He looked in on Evelyn and found her sitting up in bed reading a magazine.

"Hi," she said cheerily. "Lovely day, isn't it?"

"How're you feeling?" he asked.

"Not bad. How about you?"

"So-so. Like something to eat?"

"Love something. I'm famished. But don't trouble yourself, David. I'll get it." She started to get up, then winced and slumped back onto the bed. "Guess I'm not as chipper as I thought I was. Maybe you'd better get it after all."

He hunted up a can of tomato soup and some crackers. Back in the bedroom he set a bowl of soup and crackers on a tray across her lap and put another for himself on the end table near the window.

"Good," she purred contentedly as she sampled it. Then smiling wanly she said, "I suppose we've got to talk about this sooner or later, so we might as well talk about it now. I'm sorry, of course. I realize what trouble I must've put you through. I wish I hadn't. Beyond that, I don't know what to say. Frankly, it frightens me just to think about it."

"Then don't think about it. Just eat your soup."

She took another spoonful. "You're being very kind and considerate, David. I want you to know I appreciate it."

"Think nothing of it."

"I also want you to know I've learned my lesson."

His eyebrows arched hopefully.

She smiled. "I won't be bothering you any more, David. It was foolish of me to think you had any feelings toward me other than as a convenient and willing sex object—"

"Don't say that, Evelyn. I've had fond feelings toward you."

"You needn't be gallant, David. I understand." Her

smile was that of the abdicating queen graciously surrendering to the commanding general of the revolutionary army. "Suffice it to say that I won't tax your patience any longer. As soon as I finish this soup I'll get up and get dressed and be on my way. You'll never have to–" She broke off as the phone rang.

Dave started to reach for the instrument on the night table, then decided to take the call out in the living room. "Be right back," he said.

Evelyn Draper's smile broadened. "Take your time, David. Believe me, I've learned my lesson. You have nothing to worry about with me any more."

She waited until he closed the door behind him. Then she counted ten and carefully lifted the receiver of the bedside phone and put it to her ear.

"Tobie!" she heard David exclaim.

"I'm sorry I gave you such a rough time yesterday, darling," Tobie Williams replied. "I hated myself afterwards. I tried to phone you last night, but there was no answer. Will you be free tonight after your show?"

He hesitated. Frank Dewan had said to give Evelyn plenty of attention and to make sure not to let her feel rejected. But if she was telling the truth a few minutes ago, all his troubles were over. "Sure," he said. "Shall I come to your place?"

Tobie chuckled. "Not just yet, Dave. Roomie problems again. Anjelica moved out and Madolyn–that's the replacement–is moving in."

He groaned.

"But it's strictly temporary, darling. I've made my decision. I'm willing to do it your way."

"You mean move in with me?"

"Whenever you want me to."

He started to say "Tonight." Then he remembered Evelyn Draper in his bedroom. "Great," he said instead. "We'll work out the details tonight. I'll see you at the Sardine Factory at one."

When he returned to the bedroom, Evelyn was slumped back against the pillow, seemingly asleep, the soup tray still on her lap. He went to the side of the bed and took the tray. As he did, she began to toss fitfully and to whimper, "Help me, help me, help me."

"Wake up, Evelyn," he said, gently shaking her.

"No, no," she continued to whimper, tossing more violently. "I have nobody. Won't somebody help me?"

"Evelyn," he commanded, "wake up!"

Her eyes flew open, and she stared at him with an expression of near-terror.

"What is it?" he asked.

She buried her face in the pillow. "Go away, go away." She began to sob hysterically. "Oh, God, I wish I were dead."

He sat next to her. "What is it? Tell me what's wrong."

She turned her face away from him and replied in a barely audible voice, "I had a dream. I was drowning in the ocean, and you were standing there watching. I reached out for you, and you just stood there."

"It was just a dream. It's all over now." He patted her shoulder. "Don't worry, you're going to be fine."

She seemed not to hear him. "Oh, God," she said, shuddering. "I'm so alone." She looked at him entreatingly. "Please, David. Hold me. Just for a little while."

In spite of himself, he felt pity for the pale, forlorn figure staring up at him. He held out his arms and she snuggled into them.

"Tighter," she whispered. "Tighter, David. Don't let me go."

He held her tighter, gently rocking her shoulders as he patted her back. Maybe, he told himself, he had been premature in accepting her word earlier when she said that she was ready to go home. "Evelyn," he asked, "would you like me to cancel tonight's show and stay here with you?"

She slowly looked up at him and smiled demurely. "That's very sweet of you, David. But it won't be necessary. I'm afraid I'm a little too weak to go home just now, but I'm sure I'll feel stronger later. Why don't you do the show, then give me a ride home afterwards?"

He hesitated, wondering how he would explain to Tobie—especially if Evelyn decided once they were home that she wanted company for the entire night. But he remembered Frank Dewan's warning. "Okay, Evelyn," he said, "that's what we'll do."

She snuggled up against him. "You're so considerate, David. Really. I love you so much." Quickly she added, "But I won't give you any more trouble. I promise. After tonight—I swear to you, David, criss-cross my heart and hope to die—you'll never hear from me again."

He said nothing.

"Would you like that—not hearing from me any more?"

"Let's not talk about it just now, Evelyn. Right now, let's just get some rest so we'll both be nice and strong and relaxed when it's time to go."

He slid down in the bed and she automatically fitted her body into place against his. A few minutes later, the regular rhythm of her breathing told him that she was sleeping.

He lay silently with her for almost an hour. Then he gently lifted her arm from his chest and quietly left the room. He had to phone Tobie to cancel their date at the Sardine Factory.

He dialed her number and listened with a sick feeling as the phone rang ten, fifteen, then twenty times without an answer. Evidently she had left for the night and wouldn't be back until after her date with him.

"David!" Evelyn suddenly cried, bursting into the living room. "Oh," she said as she spotted him, "I—I woke up and you were gone."

He quietly replaced the receiver in its cradle. Evelyn, he saw, was trembling violently. Her face was almost chalk-white.

"If you have something planned for tonight," she said, "you can take me home now. I'm a little weak, but I think I'll hold up okay."

He stared at her. Her eyes had a look of absolute terror.

"Let her start feeling rejected once again . . ." Frank Dewan's voice warned inside Dave's head.

"I've got nothing on," he said, crossing to her. "Come on, let's go back and lie down until it's time for me to leave for the station."

NINE

"This is Dave Garland," he said into the microphone, "back at the same old stand to rap a little, read a little verse and play some music to be very, very nice to each other by."

He bled in his theme, switched off the microphone and went to the adjacent broadcast booth, where a big Ampex was cutting a duplicate of the evening's show. It would be wise to have a current dupe on hand in case he had to dash off to San Francisco for a day. Al Monte or one of the other jocks could play it in his absence and the listeners wouldn't be any the wiser.

He adjusted the record level on the Ampex, then went back to the console. The light on one of the phones was flashing.

"Let's start things out with one for the silent majority," he said, bleeding out his theme and readying the record on the other turntable. "The year is nineteen thirty-eight, the place Carnegie Hall, the band Benny Goodman, the trumpet Ziggy Elman—what else but, *And the Angels Sing?*"

He released the record, flicked off the microphone and picked up the telephone. "KRML, Dave Garland."

"Hi, darling," said Evelyn Draper. "How are you?"

He tensed, certain that some new disaster lay just ahead. "Are you all right?"

"Of course. I feel fine." She chuckled softly.

"Well?" He waited. "I take it you didn't call just to tell me you feel fine."

"Of course not, darling. Don't get uptight." Baby-talking, she added, "Poor David, he always gets so uptight when things happen unexpectedly, doesn't he?"

"Evelyn," he said impatiently, "I'm on the air—"

"I know, darling. I'm lying here listening to you. That's why I called. Will you do it one last time?"

"Do *what* one last time?" he half-shouted exasperatedly.

"Play *Misty* for me, of course." Her chuckle blossomed into a laugh. "After all, David, it is our song. And this is our last night together, just as I promised. Don't you think it's fitting that you—"

"Yes, sure. I have the album right here on the playrack. I'll cue it up now."

"Thank you, darling. I'll be listening. 'Bye."

The phone call reminded him that he had to cancel his date with Tobie Williams. He cued up the album, then dialed her number. Still no answer. He considered going to the Sardine Factory for a few minutes after the show: he could meet her, explain the situation, then—

No. The explanation—if Tobie believed it—would take more time than he had. He couldn't risk leaving Evelyn back at his place feeling rejected. Not when the end was so close in sight.

What he'd do was continue phoning Tobie at home until the show was over, just on the chance she might come back. And if he didn't reach her by one, he'd leave a message for her with Murphy at the Sardine Factory.

In fact, it wouldn't be a bad idea to leave the message with Murphy now—just in case it should slip his mind as he got wrapped up in the show.

He started to dial the Sardine Factory, but stopped after four digits. Ziggy Elman, on turntable two, was ripping to the end of the sock chorus of *And the Angels Sing.* Dave fumbled with the book of poetry that he had planned to read from, decided he didn't have time to hunt for his page and switched on the microphone just as Ziggy Elman attacked his final high E-flat.

"Eight-oh-seven p.m., and I'm Dave Garland. Here's a pretty tune for lonely lovers on a foggy night: Errol Garner and *Misty.*" He bled in the Garner piano, then leaned closer to the mike and said in a near-whisper, "This is especially for Evelyn. Music to say farewell by."

Flicking off the mike, he leaned back in his chair

and sighed mightily. Farewell, indeed. And good riddance. Just as soon as he got her home tonight.

Now, if only he could manage to get her there without further trouble!

He should have realized, of course, that he wouldn't.

When he got back to his apartment after the show, he found her sitting cross-legged on the floor in front of the fireplace. She was wearing a floor-length, finely pleated culotte and a matching long-sleeved blouse which tied between her breasts, exposing her midriff and a great deal of cleavage. Errol Garner's *Misty* album was on the stereo.

"Hi," she purred demurely, rising to greet him. "I missed you." She stepped into his arms and tilted her mouth to be kissed.

"I see you're feeling better."

"Much." She pirouetted away from him, causing the harem-like pants of her culotte to balloon out. "You haven't told me how sexy I look."

"You look ravishing. Are you ready to go?"

She frowned. "The lady at the store guaranteed that you'd flip."

"What lady at what store?"

"The lady at the store where I bought these."

"You went out shopping tonight?"

"Of course not, idiot. Yesterday. When I bought *Misty*." She gestured toward the stuffed cerise dog, which was propped up against the fireplace. "And a few other things for our date that didn't come off."

"Uh, Evelyn—I thought that we weren't going to do any more of this. I thought I was going to come back from the station and give you a ride home and that'd be the end of it."

"Wait a minute." She spun around and removed a pair of men's slippers from a shoe box on the table next to the wall. "Surprise!" she cried, holding them up in front of him.

He said nothing.

She pouted. "Well, don't you like them?"

"They're fine, but–" His voice trailed off. In his mind he could hear Frank Dewan's voice saying, "Humor her. Play along with her–at least until you get her out of your apartment."

"Don't spoil my fun, darling," she pleaded. "I love to give you things." Suddenly she dropped to her knees in front of him. "It's Madame Butterfly time. First, friendly neighborhood geisha remove honorable shoes." She reached for them.

"Stop it!" Abruptly, almost violently, he jerked away from her. Frank Dewan's voice was pleading with him to play her game. But he couldn't play it any longer.

"What's the matter?" she asked, seeming very hurt.

"Get up, Evelyn. We have to talk."

"Have I done something wrong?"

"You've done everything wrong."

She moved toward him, still on her knees, and reached for his waist.

"Look, Evelyn," he said, his voice tight with exasperation, "I'm trying to be straight with you."

"Be straight with somebody else, David. Be nice to me." She wrapped her arms around his thighs and pressed her cheek against his crotch.

He silently reached down and disengaged her grip.

"I don't understand, David. Are you trying to say you don't love me any more?"

"Any more?" He stared at her incredulously. "I never said I loved you, Evelyn. Never."

"Not in words, perhaps. But, oh, David, there are ways of saying things that have nothing whatsoever to do with words."

Frank Dewan's urgings were loud in his ears, but Dave couldn't force himself to heed them. "Come off it, Evelyn," he snapped. "I never gave you the slightest indication I was in love with you."

"It's that other bitch, isn't it?"

"What are you talking about?"

"The little blonde pussycat in the picture on your dresser. She's the one, isn't she?"

"Never mind her. Just get up and put your coat on, because I'm driving you home."

"After all this? After I went through the trouble of buying my outfit just so you'd like it, and—"

"Enough, Evelyn! I can't take it any more, baby!" His jaws suddenly were clenched tight and his balled-up fist quivered menacingly inches from her face. "I've had it with you, Evelyn. Now, goddam it, get up and get your ass out of here before you make me do something we'll both regret!"

She shrank back, seeming genuinely frightened. Then, slowly, a small smile played across her lips. Evenly she said, "The worst possible thing you could do to me, David, is send me away. Beat me up, if it makes you feel better. I don't mind. Do anything you want to me. But don't send me away."

He felt the tightness drain out of his muscles as he faced her in impotent rage.

"And you won't send me away," she continued. "You know what trouble I could cause for you, if I wanted to. That's why you didn't report me to the police last night. You've got pussycat in there–" she gestured vaguely toward the bedroom–"on a string and you've got that San Francisco job in the works and you're not going to do anything that'll screw either of them up."

"Are you blackmailing me?" he asked, weak with weariness and disgust.

"That's as good a word as any, I suppose. Whatever you call it, you're going to make love to me tonight–whether you want to or not. And you're going to do it again in the future, if I want you to. Which I will. So you might as well face up to it, Buster Blue Eyes: I'm with you for the duration. You are not–repeat, not–going to dump me."

Silently he went to the telephone and lifted the receiver.

"Who are you calling?" she asked.

"The police, Evelyn. You're a very disturbed girl. You need help. I can't give it to you. Maybe they can."

"You wouldn't dare call them. It'd mean the end of your career."

He silently dialed nine-one-one.

"You're bluffing, David," she hissed. "You're trying to scare me."

He turned away. Suddenly he could not bear to look at her for another second.

"Police headquarters, Sergeant Price," said the voice on the other end of the phone.

"Sergeant, my name is Dave Garland—"

What happened next took place in seconds but seemed to stretch out over days and days.

Somewhere behind him as he gave his name to the police sergeant, Dave heard a scuffling sound. It somehow seemed threatening and ominous.

He turned quickly, but not quickly enough. Evelyn Draper was over him. She seemed suspended in air, like a lion leaping on its prey. In her hand was something big and cylindrical, maybe a bottle, maybe a club of some kind—though he could not imagine where she could have gotten it.

The receiver of the phone was still at his ear. "Yes, Mister Garland?" he heard the sergeant say. The voice was clear and calm and seemed totally removed—worlds-away removed—from the strange thing that was happening here in the living room of his own apartment.

He knew that Evelyn was swinging this big, cylindrical thing toward his head. He knew that he would have to block it in some way. But, though the thing seemed to descend with glacial slowness, he somehow could not raise his arms more quickly.

On the other end of the wire now was the electric sound of a live telephone connection. The police sergeant had finished saying 'Yes, Mister Garland?' and was waiting for a reply.

But Dave could say nothing. His mouth opened with the same incredible slowness that his blocking forearm was rising and, meanwhile, the cylindrical thing that Evelyn Draper was swinging at his head was descending with equal slowness—all three things happening at the same speed, but the cylindrical thing's descent having begun first, therefore, the culmination of its movement seemed to occur first. . . .

How weird, he found himself thinking, as, in a seemingly distant part of his mind, he contemplated the three forces very neatly fulfilling their choreographed roles. It's almost like watching a slow motion film of a ballet. . . .

And then the cylindrical thing struck.

It hit him on the head and he felt himself toppling to the floor, the telephone receiver tumbling from his grip.

And, as if from leagues away, light-years away, he heard the sergeant's voice saying, "Mister Garland? Mister Garland?"

And Evelyn Draper, somewhere in the background, was saying, "Sorry, sergeant, my boyfriend is a practical joker." Click.

And Dave felt himself standing on his head—or so it seemed—and then tumbling, his weight all on one shoulder, then on his back, now on his side, now on his face.

And somewhere else in the distance someone seemed to be trying to tell him something—someone he didn't recognize, although the voice sounded like Johnny Murphy's—telling him something about Dave's having forgotten to leave a message for Tobie at the Sardine Factory, which meant that she would be waiting there for him now and he would stand her up . . .

And then the voice faded and the sensation of tumbling faded and all other awarenesses faded and there was only a weird, thick, misty blackness.

TEN

He was awakened by the sound of a woman's voice. "Stone cold dead in the market!" she cried vehemently.

Dave opened one eye and stared balefully at a tall, attractive black woman of about forty, with a natural haircut and humorous eyes.

"Remember me?" she asked. "I'm the lady who comes in to clean three times a week." She surveyed him from head to toe, then added, "But removing dead bodies isn't part of my job. You want to die, get somebody else to come haul you away."

Dave groaned. His head was throbbing violently; he felt it would split if he moved a quarter of an inch. "Go away, Birdie," he murmured.

"It must have been quite a party," she continued, picking up the vodka bottle that lay on the floor alongside his head. "Having so much fun you didn't even get around to opening this one, huh?" She put it on a shelf, then began wandering around the room, peering into corners. "Any other bodies?" she called cheerfully. "Any other zonked juiceheads around here?"

"Birdie," he pleaded, "come back later. Like tomorrow. Or next year."

She ignored him. Crossing toward the bedroom, she said, "Better check the old work bench." She poked her head inside and called loudly, "All right, break it up in here!"

Dave suddenly remembered Evelyn Draper, who, having beaned him with the vodka bottle, presumably was still somewhere in the general vicinity. He lifted himself gingerly from the floor and moved past Birdie into the bedroom. "Evelyn?" he called.

Birdie followed him. "Lose something, tiger?"

He checked the bathroom. "Evelyn?"

Birdie watched bemusedly for a moment, then parodied his search. "Evelyn?" She looked into the closet. "Evelyn?" She lifted a pillow.

"Birdie," he said, "couldn't you find it in your heart to come back some other time?"

"This is some other time, pussycat. I'm paying you back for that day you threw me out last week." She opened a drawer. "Evelyn?" Turning back to Dave, she said, "What I can't figure out is, with action in *here*, what're you doing sleeping out *there* on the floor."

He pointed to the lump on his head. "I fell afoul of a crazy woman, Birdie—and not in the way you might think."

"Ach soooo. Which explains why the bottle was full. Well, sit yourself down, big fella, and I'll see if I can hunt up some aspirin and an icepack. And–" She almost jumped as the phone on the night table rang with what, in view of Dave's condition, seemed sadistic loudness. "I'll get it," she said, scooping up the receiver. "We may be on the rocks around here, but we've still got some class." Into the mouthpiece she said, "Mister Garland's residence." She listened for a moment, then cupped her hand over the mouthpiece and whispered, "Do you want to talk to a Madge Brenner?"

He nodded and took the receiver.

"Dave, darling!" gushed the voice at the other end of the wire. "I must tell you how much I enjoyed your tape. I'd heard good things about you, of course, and I'd listened to part of your show one night when I was in Carmel. But listening to the whole tape was an actual experience, darling–you're so smooth, so forceful, so–" she paused and lowered her voice theatrically to a near-purr–"sexy."

"Why, thank you, Missus Brenner."

"Madge, darling. There's no room for formality between two people who are going to work as closely together as we are in the weeks and months ahead, now is there? Dave, dearest, I must tell you that I think your show is positively sensational–a whole new concept in prime time pop programming."

"Actually, Missus Br–uh, Madge–actually William B. Williams has been doing something pretty much like it in New York for the past thirty years–"

"Well, of course, Dave, there *are* similarities—superficial ones, naturally—but the point is, darling, this is not New York. It's California, Dave, don't you see? It's at the exact opposite end of the continent, my dear—three thousand miles away or thereabouts. And in any case, that's entirely irrelevant to the point of our discussion. The point, darling, is that I love your show! Now then, we must pursue this further in person—and the sooner the better. I'll fly down for lunch this afternoon. Are you free?"

"Yes—"

"All right, then, reserve a table for us in your name at the Windjammer. One o'clock should be about right. And do wear the lovely polka-dot tie you wore in that photograph you sent me. I think it brings out the fire in your eyes. Until one, then, darling—ta-ta—"

He hung up, feeling greatly relieved and wildly excited. It all seemed so close now—the job in San Francisco, marriage to Tobie—

He picked up the receiver again and dialed her number.

"This is Rita, her new roommate," said the girl who answered. "Madolyn just moved out and I'm just moving in. Tobie's over at my old apartment helping me get my things organized."

"Tell her Dave apologizes for last night and ask her to call me as soon as she gets in. I'll explain everything then."

He hung up. Tobie, he was sure, would accept his explanation. He would tell her the entire truth and she'd understand. Especially when he coupled it with the news about the San Francisco gig, now all but one hundred per cent in the bag.

Yes, everything was falling very nicely into place. All that remained was to get rid of Evelyn.

And speaking of Evelyn—

"Looks like we found her," announced Birdie, waving a note at him. "'Morning, darling,'" she read. "'Gone shopping. Back in a flash with the hash.' Little humor in there, I see. She must take lessons from your pal Monte. 'P.S., If you can't find your keys, don't worry. I borrowed your car.'"

ELEVEN

The locksmith removed the two keys from his lathe, filed the new one, then handed the pair to Evelyn Draper.

"Oh, do you work at KRML?" he asked as she fitted the old one on a key ring bearing the station's call letters.

She smiled winningly. "Yes, I'm Al Monte's secretary."

"Really? I listen to him all the time."

"Well, I'll tell him that, pardner. The stallion's always pleased to learn he's got friends out here on the range."

Chuckling amiably, she paid for the key and left the shop. But out on the street her chuckle faded and her lips curled into a small snarl.

What she should have done, she reflected bitterly, was apply for a job at the station months ago. If she had worked there as a secretary or perhaps a record librarian, David would have noticed her—she was certainly good-looking enough—and asked her out and they could have had a normal relationship.

Where she had gone wrong was in letting him pick her up at that horrible bar. How could he possibly love her after having met her under those circumstances?

Although, now that she thought of it, he might have reacted the same way if she had been sexually free after meeting him at the station, also. Conceivably it was her deviation from the old subjugated-woman stereotype that turned him off. Conceivably, he was one of those Puritan male chauvinist pigs who loves a woman only as long as she keeps her thighs closed.

Oh, well, whatever the case, his reasons for not loving her didn't matter any more. All that mattered was that she was not going to let him get away with dumping her. She was going to hold on as tight as she could and for as long as she could. And maybe, if she held on tight enough and hung around long enough, he'd see what a good thing he had going for him and fall in love with her after all. There was no reason why he shouldn't, really. After all, she was one heck of a gorgeous chick. Certainly a lot better looking than that titless blonde scatterbrain whose picture he kept in his bedroom.

Evelyn fished out one of the keys from the KRML

ring, fitted it into the ignition of the MG, and started the car with a roar. She loved driving the MG. Partly because it was a fine car, of course; but mostly because it was his. Damn it, she loved everything connected with him, handsome and sexy rat that he was.

She wished she hadn't hit him so hard with that vodka bottle last night. When he fell unconscious, she thought for a moment that she might have killed him. He lay so absolutely still and his face got so white! Fortunately, she had had the presence of mind to check his pulse and had found that it was still beating strongly. If he had died, she didn't know what she would do. Probably she would have had to do something awful and grisly, like dismember the body and dispose of it piece by piece in an incinerator. She certainly couldn't afford to leave the corpse around. Not after Monte and the guy from the Sardine Factory and who-knew-who-else had seen her in David's company.

Well, happily enough, he had not died. She had applied cold compresses to his face and, before long, his color had come back and he was sleeping as peacefully as if he were in bed. In fact, she had thought of waking him and taking him to bed, but she realized that he'd be pretty angry after all she had done to him. So she left him there on the floor and slept alone in his bed.

When she awakened at eight in the morning, he was still sleeping peacefully—though he had an egg-sized lump on his head, poor guy. She checked his pulse again, then went through his pockets and found his keys. As she thought back on it, she had to admit that she had been pretty afraid while she was doing it. Suppose he woke up and found her searching him? In fact, he almost did wake up; several times during the search he stirred and seemed about to open his eyes. Fortunately, he always went right back to sleep.

Once the keys were securely tucked away in her purse, she wrote him a note saying that she was going shopping. Then she left the apartment, drove to her own apartment, changed clothes, stopped at a supermarket for some groceries and had the key to his apartment duplicated by the locksmith.

No doubt, he'd be furious when she got back. But she'd figure out some way to handle him, just as she always had in the past. And in any case, the main thing was that she now had the duplicate key. She'd never have to plead with him again to let her in to use the bathroom!

She pulled the MG to a halt in his driveway, let herself into the apartment with the duplicate key—just to make sure it worked before returning his key ring—then pocketed it and brought the groceries into the kitchen. She noticed as she crossed the living room that he was no longer on the floor and that the place had been tidied up a bit.

"David?" she called.

He came out of the bedroom, wearing suit pants and a dark, long-sleeved shirt. He was tying a thick windsor knot in a dark, polka-dotted tie.

"My, my," she beamed, looking at him admiringly, "don't we look nice all gussied up?"

His jaws clenched in anger as he extended his hand, palm upward. "Give me the keys, Evelyn," he said in a voice that was more menacing because of its softness.

She cheerfully dropped the KRML key ring into his palm. "Actually, David, I'm glad you're dressed up. I was going to cook us some brunch, but suddenly I'm in the mood for something more festive." She smiled brightly. "How about the Butcher Shop? My treat. After all I put you through, it's the least I can–"

"I'm having lunch with somebody."

"Business?"

"None of yours." He noticed her beginning to frown. He quickly reminded himself that if he could just keep her at bay for another day or so–just long enough to get the San Francisco deal squared away with Madge Brenner and to explain everything to Tobie–he'd be home free. "Actually, Evelyn," he added hastily, "I am having a business lunch. But I wish you wouldn't ask personal questions. It's very annoying. Now wait here just a second while I get my jacket, then I'll drop you off at your apartment on the way to my appointment."

"No need to bother." She went to the telephone. "I think I'll have lunch downtown and buy a pair of shoes. I'll call a cab."

"You're sure you're strong enough–I mean, after losing all that blood?"

"I'm just fine, David. I swear, I've never felt better."

Well, I hope you always feel that way, baby, he thought as he retreated to the bedroom for his jacket.

And I hope the earth opens up in front of you on your way home and you fall inside.

He put on his jacket, gave his hair another once-over with a comb, checked the knot of his tie, then went upstairs to the terrace where Birdie was hanging clothes and told her to tell all telephone callers that he'd be back late in the afternoon.

When he returned to the living room, Evelyn was just leaving. "I'll be seeing you," she called as she hurried to the taxi at the curb.

"No way," he said under his breath, telling himself that he'd take a salary cut if need be to hasten the signing of Madge Brenner's contract.

But, of course, no such sacrifice would be necessary. Judging from the way she sounded on the phone, Madge Brenner would accept just about any terms he chose to dictate.

And that meant San Francisco and marriage to Tobie just as soon as humanly possible.

He vaulted over the side of the MG, started the motor and pulled smoothly out of the driveway. As he moved into the downtown traffic, he whistled, *San Francisco, Open Your Golden Gate* . . .

Yes, he told himself ecstatically, after dealing him more than a few bum hands, the law of averages was finally wiring him with aces.

So pleased was he with the current turn of events that he did not even bother to think as he glanced through his rear-view mirror and saw Evelyn Draper in the taxi behind him that, having left a full minute or two before him, the most logical explanation for her being where she was now was that she was following him.

TWELVE

The maitre d' escorted him to a window table where a handsome woman of fifty-five with penetrating blue eyes and extremely well-coiffed white hair sat sipping a dry sherry.

"Dave, darling!" beamed Madge Brenner, rising as he approached. "How lovely you look—and, mercy me, you've worn the tie I like so well. How sweet of you, darling. How positively divine. But don't let me keep you standing, dearest. Do sit and have this nice man bring you one of those drinks he makes so expertly."

Dave ordered a straight scotch with a water chaser, then sat back and studied Madge Brenner as her torrent of words continued.

There was about her, he mused, the unmistakable scent of money; she wore it the way other women wear perfume. There also was no disguising her sexual appreciation of him. But while her ice-blue eyes more than once darted over his body and then fixed to his, and while she larded her sentences with darlings and dearests, she had a dignity and self-confidence about her that didn't jibe with the classic image of an old lady on the make. Madge Brenner had, in a word, class.

She also had a thorough knowledge of radio. She might favor a gushy conversational style, à la Rosalind Russell in *Auntie Mame*, but it was obvious after just a few minutes' conversation with her that she was not one of the West's leading station managers by fluke. She was a woman of great intelligence and business acumen who could neither be fooled nor taken in by flattery.

Accordingly, Dave set himself to the task of making her respect his professionalism while admiring his person and enjoying his personality. He knew that he had succeeded when, over coffee, she gave him the card of a San Francisco lawyer and said, "Have your attorney contact ours to work out the details, darling. We'll be ready for you as soon as these legal minds can get together." If she just thought him an ordinary deejay looking for a job, she would have offered him her station's form contract on a take-it-or-leave-it basis.

"And now, darling," she said as the waiter brought snifters of brandy, "let us drink to the inevitable success of San Francisco's Dave Garland Show—an exciting new concept in . . ." She broke off and her face froze in an expression of bewilderment as she looked up from the table.

Dave followed her gaze and found himself looking at Evelyn Draper. She stood over the table, her fists on her hips. Her eyes burned. "Well, isn't this cozy?" she sneered.

Dave's jowls bulged in anger. Madge Brenner glanced, astonished, from Evelyn to him and back to Evelyn.

"So this is your business appointment?" Evelyn turned to Madge. "Well, sweetie, how's business?"

Madge looked to Dave for an explanation.

Evelyn answered for him, "I'm just another trick, honey. I guess he got his signals crossed."

Other diners turned to stare as Dave rose and took her by the elbow. "That's enough, Evelyn," he said, trying to lead her away.

She shook her arm free. "Is this your idea of a groovy chick?" she demanded. "She's a little old for you, baby, don't you think?" A demoniacal smile flickered across her face. "I've got it—this is Be-Kind-to-Senior-Citizens-Week, is that right?"

"Let's go, Evelyn," Dave said grimly, again trying to steer her away.

She grabbed the tablecloth for leverage. "It's not that I mind your being a bastard, David. But do you have to be such a tasteless bastard? This broad couldn't get laid in a lumber camp."

Dave felt his anger rise like erupting lava. "Out!!!" he roared, wresting Evelyn's hand from the tablecloth.

Several dishes fell to the floor, their clatter only

partially muffling Evelyn's outraged cry, "You're hurting me, you two-timing son of a bitch!"

Dave threw a despairing glance at Madge, who sat staring straight ahead, her face a mask. Then he grabbed Evelyn by the shoulders and half-pushed, half-dragged her out of the restaurant.

As they reached the street he spotted an empty taxi and gestured to the driver. "Let me go, you dirty pig bastard, let me go!" Evelyn shouted, fighting to break away from him.

As passersby stopped and stared, Dave opened the cab door and pushed her inside. "Take her anywhere," he told the driver, stuffing a ten dollar bill into the man's hand, "just get her out of here."

"Yes, sir!" said the driver.

"Don't you dare, you prick!" Evelyn shouted. Then, as the cab lurched forward, her expression changed and she looked imploringly at Dave.

"I'm sorry, darling! Please forgive me! I promise it'll never hap–" Her words faded as the cab shot away from the curb.

Dave felt suddenly weak. Lifelessly he went back into the restaurant, ignoring the crowd which had gathered on the sidewalk and in the doorway. He reached Madge Brenner's table just as she was paying the check.

"Please don't leave, Madge," he said. "I can explain everything."

"I'm afraid, Mister Garland," she replied icily, "that an explanation would be entirely superfluous."

"But, Madge–Missus Brenner–"

"*Mister* Garland, when I became interested in you, I assumed that you conducted your personal life with the sort of propriety and decorum which is the hallmark of civilized people everywhere. This obviously is not the case, and frankly, Mister Garland, there is no room at my station for a disc jockey who, for whatever reasons there may be, provokes displays of the sort I have witnessed this afternoon." She snatched up the card of her station's attorney, which Dave had left on the table next to his brandy snifter. "You won't be needing this, I'm afraid," she said with unmistakable finality as she turned and stalked away.

Dave, watching her, found that in that tiny corner of his brain where thinking was still possible he knew that those wired aces were only the law of averages setting him up to be sandbagged.

THIRTEEN

"I ninety-five per cent believe you," said Tobie Williams.

Dave watched her stare out at the ocean. They sat on her balcony, listening to the breakers a hundred feet below crash thunderingly against the palisades. He waited for her to continue, but she fell silent. "What's the five per cent that you don't believe?" he asked finally.

"I don't know." She seemed suddenly to become fascinated with the fabric of her slacks. Staring intently at them, she said, "I believe there's a broad named Evelyn. I believe she screwed up your meeting with Madge Brenner. I guess I believe that she tried to commit suicide in your apartment. And that there never was anything between you but sex. And that the only reason you put up with her these past few days was because you were afraid of what she'd do if you didn't."

"Well? What's left to disbelieve?"

She shook her head. "I don't know, Dave. I honestly don't. I only know that when you didn't show up at the Sardine Factory, I got that old-time feeling of jealousy and mistrust."

"And you're going to let that keep you from moving in with me?"

"Not forever, Dave. Hopefully just for a little while longer."

He tried to say something, but he was at a loss for words. He paced the balcony and finally stopped at one of the outside corners. He put his foot on the rail and stared silently out at the turbulent ocean.

After a moment she came to him and put her arms around his waist from behind. "I'm sorry, darling. I'm not trying to give you a hard time. It's just that, when I move in with you, I don't plan to move out unless you throw me out. So before I do move in, I've got to be positive I'm ready. Ninety-five per cent positive isn't enough."

He said nothing, but gently covered her hands with his.

"And there's really no hurry, is there? Especially now that the San Francisco gig has fallen through. I mean, you'll be in Carmel and I'll be in Carmel and we can see each other whenever you like."

"Yeah. Just you and me and the roommate of the month."

"We've been through that before, Dave. You know it can't be any other way."

He realized that she was right. In his urgency to be assured of her love, he was doing the one thing that unfailingly turned him off when a girl did it to him: he was holding on too tight. "Okay, Tobe." He turned to her and made himself smile. "We'll do it your way."

"I love you, Dave," she said, stepping into his arms and offering her mouth. "I always have."

"I love you, darling," he said, kissing her.

Evelyn Draper, watching them through binoculars from the public lookout point half a mile down the road, naturally did not hear their expressions of endearment. But she sensed what they were saying and, as she watched their bodies come together, a tight knot formed in the pit of her stomach.

Why should Dave Garland be in love with this skinny blonde instead of with Evelyn?

What did Tobie Williams have that Evelyn Draper did not?

Hadn't Evelyn offered him everything? Hadn't she proved that there was nothing she would refuse to do to make him happy?

Why wouldn't he accept what she wanted to give him?

Through her binoculars she saw Dave and Tobie walk toward the house, then vanish inside. The knot in her stomach tightened. Now they would make love. But he shouldn't be making love to Tobie Williams. He should be making love to Evelyn Draper!

Her mouth dry with rage, her eyes pinpricks of hate,

Evelyn got into her car and started up the coastal road. She had no particular destination. She wanted only to lose her fury, to burn it out, to drive it away.

She drove past the Carmel exit, then past the next three, picking up speed at each. The needle on her speedometer jerked past eighty, then eighty-five, then ninety.

A new Mercury that looked as though it wouldn't outlive its warranty was plodding along in the lane ahead and a Pontiac was making a leisurely pass. She drew closer to them, closer still. If she didn't slow down, and right away, there was sure to be a crash. But she kept the accelerator pressed to the floor.

She'd make it a game, she decided. A game of the sort she used to play with herself in grade school. Close your eyes and put the point of your pencil on the page of your spelling book. If it lands on a word, you'll pass tomorrow's test. If it lands on white space, you'll fail.

Today's game would have higher stakes and greater risks. It would be a game of chicken. She'd continue to speed straight toward the cars and would lean on her horn to warn them out of her way. If she kept her nerve and the cars did get out of her way, her reward would be Dave Garland: he would decide that he had been wrong in turning her away and he would ask her to come back to him. If she chickened out and took her foot from the accelerator, she would lose him to Tobie Williams for good.

Her pulse pounded as she raced toward the cars, now seeming to magnify themselves in jump-cuts as she drew closer. Her horn was loud in her ears—but the drivers ahead evidently did not hear it, because they stayed on course.

Closer.

Closer.

Dangerously close now.

Almost fatally close.

Suddenly, as if on cue, both drivers seemed to react. The Pontiac shot ahead, belching black fumes from its exhaust as the driver kicked in his passing gear. The lazy Mercury at the same time edged toward the shoulder.

But it wasn't happening fast enough. She had too much momentum. She was almost on top of them.

Screeeeehhhhh!!!!!

The sound of her brakes was like a siren as her car jerked and dipped from the impact. The Mercury managed to get off the road just in time. She wobbled past, almost sideswiping the Pontiac, then released her brakes and guided her car onto the open highway ahead.

Her pulse was throbbing; her knees were literally quivering. It had been a very close scrape.

And, damn it, she had lost the game—and David!

Her rage came back, stronger, fiercer, as if he had been responsible for her near-accident. Almost blind with fury, she pulled to the left lane, slowed to thirty, then executed a skidding U-turn across the median.

As her wheels took hold on the pavement, she smiled grimly. David was going to pay dearly for his sins.

Slowly and purposefully she drove back to Carmel. She let herself into his apartment with her duplicate key, then went to the medicine chest in his bathroom and took a blade from the pack in the box with his razor.

His polka-dot tie was draped over the back of a chair. She slowly slit it lengthwise, peeling the outer cloth away to expose gauze-like innards. Then she ripped the innards out and cut the rest of the tie into fine shreds.

Next she went to his closet and carefully cut ribbon-like strips down the fronts of two suit jackets. The razor blade, she suddenly decided, was not efficient. It didn't cut deep enough and holding it made her hands sore. She rummaged around until she found a large scissors, then went back to work, cutting gashes in the backs and sides of jackets, severing sleeves, mutilating lapels, slashing trousers.

With slowly mounting fury, she worked her way through every garment in the closet, discarding them in a heap in the center of the room as she finished with them. Then she attacked the rest of the room—lampshades, drapes, curtains, bedspread. She hesitated for a moment when she thought she heard someone walking around upstairs; but she listened closely and heard no further noise, so she went back to her labors with increased vigor.

Opening bureau drawers she found shirts and socks, T-shirts and shorts, sweaters and handkerchiefs. No item escaped her. By this time her hands and wrists were almost numb from all the cutting, but she kept on, whipping herself into a near frenzy.

Finally, when everything cuttable in the room had been devastated, she took the photo of Tobie Williams from the night table, smashed the glass over the bedpost, poked out the eyes of the photo with the tips of the scissors, then cut the photo to shreds.

Next she went to the living room. She mutilated the drapes and curtains, cut up the lampshades, and poked the sharp tips of the scissors through the couch and the cushions of the chairs. Then she sat in front of his record cabinet and, weeping silently, began cutting grooves with the scissor tips across the playing surface of his albums.

She had worked her way through half the collection when she heard footsteps on the stairs and looked up to find a tall, attractive black woman staring at her incredulously.

"Oh, wow!" said Birdie, surveying the room. "What on earth you doin', honey?"

Evelyn's reaction was almost instinctive. Screaming, she leaped at Birdie and went for her face with one blade of the scissors. It caught the black woman just below the eye, opening a huge gash in her cheek.

Evelyn lunged again. This time the scissor tip tore into Birdie's neck, cutting down to her collar bone.

Blood spurted fountain-like from the wounds. Birdie fell back onto the stairs, moaning. Evelyn pounced on her and continued to slash. The scissors tore gashes in Birdie's arm and breast. Evelyn did not let up.

Mustering her strength, Birdie managed to break free and start up the stairs. Evelyn lunged after her and, throwing all her weight into the blow, plunged the scissor tips into Birdie's back.

FOURTEEN

Dave noticed the crowd from a few blocks away and wondered idly why they had gathered. When he drew closer and saw the police car and ambulance, he assumed that someone in the neighborhood had had a mishap—perhaps another heart attack for old McCabe across the street.

Then he saw where the ambulance was parked, and suddenly he felt cold terror. He brought the MG to a squealing halt next to the police barricade and ran to the ambulance just as two attendants were coming out of his door carrying a stretcher.

"I heard the screams from next door," said a voice alongside him. Dave recognized Tom Miller, the man whose sleep Evelyn had disrupted that morning that now seemed so long ago.

"I called the cops," Miller continued. "Then I came

over and tried to get in to help whoever was being attacked. But the door was locked."

Dave knew who had been attacked even before the stretcher drew close enough for him to see her. "Birdie!" he gasped, rushing to her side.

Her face and body were covered with bandages. The areas around the bandages were swollen and discolored. The bandages and the sheet which was wrapped around her were stained with blood. Attached to her arm was a tube connected to a bottle of plasma, which an intern carried alongside the stretcher. Her eyes were closed.

"She said she's your cleaning lady," a policeman remarked.

Dave nodded.

Suddenly Birdie's eyes opened and the corners of her mouth rose in a weak smile. "Yeah, I'm his cleaning lady. And it's gonna cost the bum double to clean up this mess."

Dave sighed his relief that she was able to speak. "Who did it, Birdie?" he asked, holding her hand as he walked alongside the stretcher.

Another smile, but weaker; her pain obviously was intense. "I didn't get a chance to ask her name."

"Try not to talk please, ma'am," the intern said gently. The attendants lifted the stretcher to the ambulance door.

"I'll see you at the hospital, Birdie," Dave said, squeezing her hand goodbye.

"Would you come with me, Mister Garland?" the

policeman asked. "Sergeant McCallum would like to see you."

Dave followed the policeman into the apartment. A tall, burly man in his forties, who could only be a police officer, stood against the fireplace, presiding over the living room like a judge over a court. His suit was rumpled, his eyes bloodshot, his expression was one of weary resignation to the world and its ways.

"Paul McCallum, Garland," he said, offering his hand. "Suppose you tell me all about it."

Dave shook hands, then shrugged. "I just got here, sergeant."

"I'm aware you just got here, Garland. What I want you to tell me is what I'm not aware of." He ran thick fingers through the bristle-like hairs of his steel-gray crew cut. "For example, why she did it."

"Why *who* did it?"

"Your girlfriend in there." He gestured toward the bedroom.

Dave looked in, knowing full well who he would see. Evelyn Draper sat on the edge of the bed, her wrists cuffed behind her back. Her eyes were puffy and staring straight ahead. A uniformed policeman sat on the chair next to her, watching her carefully.

"For openers, sergeant, she's not my girlfriend."

McCallum took a notepad and pencil from the inside pocket of his suit. "More or less a casual acquaintance, you'd say?"

"More or less."

"Just dropped by out of the blue to hack up your

apartment and your cleaning lady. That what you're trying to tell me?"

"I'm not trying to tell you anything, sergeant."

"Well, maybe it's time you did. A lady just almost got herself killed, fella. I'm stumbling around in my stupid way trying to find out why."

"If you want hunches, mine is that she surprised your prisoner while your prisoner was wrecking the joint."

"Okay. Now why was my prisoner wrecking the joint?"

"That's a long story."

"Suppose you brew me a nice hot cup of coffee, then tell me about it."

Dave led the way into the kitchen and put a percolator on the stove.

"This Evelyn Draper," said McCallum. "Where does she come from?"

"I don't know."

"What about her family?"

"I don't know that, either. I just met her a few weeks ago. She listens to my radio show. We saw each other a few times. That's about it."

"Practically a stranger, huh?"

"Yeah."

"Then how'd she happen to have a key to your front door?"

Dave did a double-take.

McCallum smiled. "You're gonna tell me you didn't know she had it."

"Yep."

"And I'm gonna ask you how a girl who's practically a stranger could've got close enough to you to have borrowed your keys and had a duplicate made without your knowing it."

"She took my car one day to go for groceries. Maybe she had a dupe made then."

"Do you always loan your car to strangers?"

"Not always."

"Why'd you loan it to her?"

"I didn't. She took it while I was sleeping."

"That's part of the long story, huh? The implication being that she occasionally spent the night with you."

"More or less."

"The implication then being that maybe she's not such a perfect stranger."

"I never said she was perfect."

"I know what you said, Garland. What I want to know is what your relationship to her is."

"I know her casually. Met her in a bar. Came on to her. She was receptive. I balled her a few times. She fell in love with me. That's about it."

"Do girls always fall in love with you that easily?"

"Not always."

"Why did she?"

"Maybe you'd better ask her."

"Maybe I just asked you."

"I don't know why, sergeant."

"What it all boils down to is that you don't really know a hell of a lot, do you, Garland?"

"I know I'm getting pretty goddam sick of these questions."

"So am I. But they get upset with me down at the store if I don't ask 'em." McCallum gestured toward the percolator. "That coffee'd get done a lot faster if you turned on the gas."

Dave sheepishly complied.

"Now then, suppose we try it another way. Suppose you tell me everything you can about Evelyn Draper from the minute you first became aware of her existence and, if it's a good enough story, I won't have to ask you any questions at all."

Dave told the story from the beginning, not leaving anything out. When he finished, McCallum drained what was left of his second cup of coffee and put his notepad away. "Well," the police sergeant said, "that sort of squares away with everything else I've seen and heard. I'm going to book her for attempted murder, then let the D.A. knock it down to assault one. Probably they'll decide she's got a few screws loose and put her on a funny farm for a while. In any case, she shouldn't be bothering you any more—although, of course, you'll have to testify if the case goes to trial."

Dave gulped. "You mean all this? Everything I told you?"

McCallum nodded.

"My listeners will love reading about it in the papers."

"You shoulda thought of that, Garland, when you came on to her. Me, I stick like glue to my old lady, so I never have problems like this." He crossed to the door. "Thanks for the coffee." He stepped into the living room, then came back into the kitchen. "Oh, Garland—one thing more—"

Dave looked up with a smirk. "I know. Don't leave town."

"I was going to say why don't you play some Mantovani some time?"

"I didn't know you liked my program."

McCallum grinned. "I don't. I like Mantovani."

FIFTEEN

After a few weeks it seemed almost as if Evelyn Draper had never come into his life. Birdie recovered with surprising rapidity—her only really deep wound was the one in her back, and fortunately the scissors had stuck in her scapula instead of penetrating the ribs and puncturing a vital organ. The play-*Misty*-for-me calls naturally stopped coming at the station. And one afternoon when Dave and Al Monte were taping a live concert in Monterey, Madge Brenner came by to report that the San Francisco gig was not dead after all.

"I owe you an apology," she said. "It was wrong of me to blame you for something which obviously was beyond your control. I'm afraid my vanity got the better of me when that little hussy delivered her harangue." Smiling, she added, "It was the crack about lumber camps that tore it. Fact is, darling, I've always been rather large in lumber camps. Anyway, I've since managed to put my pride back together and that means that you and I are back in business. Do have your attorney contact ours, darling. The sooner the better. If they can get all those nasty details worked out in a month, I'll be able to schedule your show in my fall line-up."

Dave was strongly tempted to tell his attorney to accept whatever terms Madge Brenner's people wanted to offer. But he could not in good conscience sign a contract while Evelyn's case remained open. If she pleaded guilty there would be no problem. But if the case went to trial, the scandalous publicity might be more than Madge and her people would sit still for.

There were also, of course, Tobie's wishes to be taken into account. His relationship with her, now that Evelyn was out of the way, was going more smoothly than ever. They would meet each morning for brunch, then spend the day together in the outdoor places they loved: Hurricane Point and Lighthouse Beach, Arroyo Seco Gorge, Mack Canyon, Anderson Canyon. They would have dinner; then she would go to Jay-Jay's to work on her sculpture and he would go to the station to do his show. Afterwards they would meet at the Sardine Factory, then go back to his place to make love. Once or twice a week she would spend the night. She did not dare stay more frequently, though; her current roommate, Veronica, was afraid to stay alone in the big, spooky house on the palisades. Tobie often pointed out that she herself disliked the arrangement even more than Dave did.

"Oh, the hell with it," she said one night. "I'm tired of living my life at other people's convenience. I've made my decision. I'm going to sell the house and move in with you." Quickly she added, "That is, if the offer's still open."

He had started to say that of course it was still open. But he checked himself. "Suppose Evelyn goes to trial after you move in?" he asked. "And the papers make a big deal about my affair with her? And people point their fingers at you on the street and say—"

"I can take it."

He shook his head. "I won't let you suffer the ramifications of something you had nothing to do with, Tobe. If there's a trial and you still want to move in after it's over, the welcome mat is out. But not now."

He thought about it later and reflected that maybe he was being foolish. But he knew that he wouldn't be able to live with himself if Tobie moved in and got involved in the scandal, too.

He checked regularly with McCallum for news about the case. At a preliminary hearing, a judge ordered Evelyn held without bail pending a psychiatric examination. Then the psychiatrists ruled that she was incapable of standing trial and she was hospitalized. She disputed their decision and, at last count, her lawyer had petitioned for a bail hearing.

"I don't see how they could grant bail if the psychiatrists testify she's insane," Tobie mused.

Dave shrugged.

"Well, anyway," Tobie said, "let's look at the bright side. The sooner it all comes to a head, the sooner it'll be over. Meanwhile"—she smiled brightly—"may I spend the night at your apartment?"

His eyebrows arched questioningly. "What about Veronica?"

"She can't hack the location any more. Too far to ride to work. The agency is sending her replacement tomorrow. Her name is Annabelle."

He chuckled. "Well, let's hope she doesn't mind staying alone now and then."

That evening at the studio he picked up the phone at the start of his show and heard a familiar voice. His heart seemed to leap to his throat as she said, "Play *Misty* for me."

He tried to tell himself that it was all a mistake, a delusion. But he knew it wasn't.

"David?" she said.

It took him a while to find his own voice. "Yeah," he finally murmured.

Her tone was even, cool, self-assured. "I didn't mean to shake you up, David. I'm sorry. Pretty stupid of me to call the way I did, but I just wanted to say goodbye."

"Where are you?"

"At the airport. San Francisco. I've only got a few minutes between planes. Got a job in Hawaii."

"Do the police know?"

"I haven't escaped from jail, if that's what you're thinking." She chuckled. "I've been released. My psychiatrists said I've made great progress and I'm not sick any more. It was a nightmare, David, but now, thank goodness, it's over."

In his incredulity he could hardly think of anything to say. "Then everything is all right with you?"

"Fine, David." She chuckled again. "I only called to say goodbye and to tell you how sorry I am for everything."

"Forget it. I have."

"I hope so. Because this maiden, David—this maiden she lived with no other thought than to love and be loved by thee." She paused. "Goodbye."

The line went dead. He sat staring dumbly at the phone until the sudden silence in the room jarred him back to reality. The record on Turntable One had spun to an end.

"Cannonball Adderly," he said, hurriedly flicking on the mike. "The C-ball is making it happen these days at the Monterey Jazz Festival, along with the Duke—the Count—Joe Williams—Woody Herman—so many great ones. They'll be breaking it up Sunday night. Make it, babies. It's out of sight. And now, here's the Gabor Szabo sextette."

He started the record on Turntable Two, then turned off the mike and slouched back in his seat.

Suddenly everything was topsy-turvy. Evelyn claiming to have been released and on her way to Hawaii. How could they let her off scot-free without even a bail hearing? She had committed a major crime!

And the last thing she said on the phone: "*This maiden she lived with no other thought than to love and be loved by thee.*" The line was frighteningly familiar. He knew he had come across it—read it—recited it—dozens of times. But now, though he had a horrible feeling that she had used it for a definite purpose and that he would have to trace the line to fathom what that purpose was, his mind seemed to go blank.

He stared at the phone, which was again flashing, answered it, half expecting the caller to be Evelyn again. It wasn't; it was only an old man from Monterey who wanted to hear Artie Shaw's *Begin the Beguine.*

Dave remembered that Evelyn had asked for *Misty* also. Presumably she was out there somewhere listening for it. Almost certainly she wasn't in San Francisco.

He went to the library, pulled the appropriate Artie Shaw and Errol Garner albums and set them up on the playrack. Then he phoned Tobie and told her not to meet him after the show.

"I'm not sure Evelyn's in town, but I don't want to take any chances. She's seen your picture at my place. If she sees us together, she might follow you, find out where you live and do the same thing to you that she did to Birdie. Do you mind staying home alone tonight?"

"No. Annabelle checked in early."

"Is she there now?"

"Yes. She's up in the bedroom unpacking."

"If you want me to ask McCallum to send a cop over, I think he'll do it. I can phone him now."

"I don't think that'll be necessary, Dave. She has no way of knowing where I live. And, just for safety's sake, I'll make sure all the windows are locked along with the door."

He hesitated, wondering whether to ask her if she

could identify the line Evelyn had recited just before hanging up. He decided against it. Probably, he told himself, the line meant nothing. Probably he was letting himself get spooked because of the unexpectedness of Evelyn's call.

"Goodnight, love," he told Tobie. Then, hearing the Gabor Szabo number approach its end, he put the Errol Garner album on Turntable One and cued up *Misty*.

SIXTEEN

The song came to him in his sleep. There was no mistaking the pulsating Garner piano, no mistaking the haunting melody. He turned restlessly, trying to blot the sounds from his consciousness. He was tired and did not want to be awakened. But the song persisted, summoning him as if from a great distance.

His eyes blinked open. He listened. The realization came to him with terrifying certainty: he was not dreaming; the record was being played right now—in his apartment. He silently rolled his head slowly toward the door and tried to see into the living room. There was only blackness.

Then, suddenly, he experienced another awareness—an almost extrasensory awareness—the feeling of another body colse to his. He lifted his eyes and found himself looking into those of Evelyn Draper.

She stood over him, her arm raised above her head. Her eyes had a glazed, wild look. In her hand was the big frenching knife from his kitchen.

She stood motionless for an instant which seemed an eternity, then screamed piercingly and plunged the knife toward Dave, its tip aimed at his eye.

He rolled out of the way just in time; the knife tore into the pillow, ripping a long gash through which feathers exploded like fragments from a grenade. He reached through the swirling feathers to seize the knife, then looked up again just in time to see Evelyn vanish through the door.

Cautiously he followed her into the living room, which was coal black. Holding the knife close to his body so that she could not knock it away from him, he searched with his other hand for a lamp. He felt as if he were crossing a million miles of blackness, with every shadow harboring a threat.

Finally his fingers grazed the surface of a lamp-shade. He reached underneath and found the switch. As light flooded the room, the sudden shrill ring of the phone startled him. He spun toward it, then back toward the center of the room. The room, he gradually realized, was empty. The front door was wide open; evidently Evelyn had run out through it.

He closed the door, then answered the phone.

"Paul McCallum, Garland. Sorry to wake you. But something's come up."

"I know. She just came calling—with a butcher knife. She got away before I could stop her. She also phoned earlier tonight at the station."

"Sit tight. I'll come right over and you can tell me all about it."

He arrived within fifteen minutes. Dave poured two cups of coffee, then sat opposite him at the kitchen table.

"They released her on bail," McCallum said. "Her lawyer was an on-the-ball guy who pressed for a quick hearing. He also drew a judge who was either soft-headed or tit-happy: he let her go for a bondsman's fee of two hundred dollars."

"When did it all happen? This afternoon?"

"Two days ago."

"Well, thanks a lot, old buddy. I mean, I really appreciate the way you broke your ass to let me know about it."

"I just found out myself."

"Great. Wonderful. Who's in charge here?"

"Look. You want to help find her, or would you rather just sit around and bellyache about it?"

"Okay. I want to help."

McCallum leaned back in his chair, took a huge swallow of coffee and smacked his lips. "Now what exactly did she say when she phoned you at the station?"

Dave recounted the conversation. McCallum's eyebrows rose as Dave repeated her last line.

"'Thee?'" the police sergeant echoed. "Is she a Quaker?"

"The line is from a poem."

"What poem?"

"I don't remember."

"A pretty old one, I'd guess. They don't write 'thee' in too many poems nowadays, do they?"

"No."

"Do you figure she was trying to tell you something by it?"

"Yeah. It bothered me when I heard it. She was trying to tell me something, but I go blank whenever I try to tune in on what."

"Who wrote the poem? Maybe that'd be a clue."

"I don't remember. Sometimes I seem to be so close I can touch him, but then I lose the name."

"How does the line go again?"

"*This maiden she lived with no other thought than to love and be loved by thee.*"

"Do you have one of those quotations books that lists sayings by topic? Maybe you could find it under 'maiden.' "

"I have one down at the station. I should've thought of it before I left."

McCallum sipped his coffee. "I'm certainly no expert on poetry, having scrupulously avoided it since a fifth grade teacher made me memorize James Russell Lowell's *The First Snowfall.* But judging from the sound of the line your girl used, I'd say the poem was maybe sixteenth or seventeenth century, huh?"

Dave shook his head. "A lot later than that. Nineteenth, probably. The rhythm is more like Coleridge or Poe—" He stopped short and his face suddenly became animated. "Poe! Of course!"

McCallum smiled; his stratagem for jolting Dave's memory had worked perfectly.

"That's why it seemed so familiar," Dave continued. "I've read the son of a bitch a hundred times on my show:

"It was many and many a year ago,
"In a kingdom by the sea
"That a maiden there lived whom you may know
"By the name of Annabel Lee;
"And this maiden she lived with no other thought
"Than to love and be loved by me.
"I was a child and she was a child,
"In this kingdom by the sea,
"But we loved with a love that was more than love—
"I and my Annabel Lee."

He looked at McCallum. "Well," asked the police sergeant, "where does that leave us?"

Dave's face clouded. "We just lost our one and only clue. I know what she was trying to tell me and it doesn't help us a bit."

"What was she trying to tell you?"

"The night she attempted suicide, she threatened that she was never going to let me go. She quoted Edgar Allan Poe's poem, *The Raven*, where the bird refuses to leave the guy. *Take thy beak from out my heart, take thy form from off my door! Quoth the Raven, 'Nevermore!'* "

"So you figure she quoted *Annabel Lee* now to remind you that she quoted *The Raven* then?"

"That's about it."

"Seems like kind of a round-about way of going at it, doesn't it?"

"She's a kind of round-about chick."

McCallum shook his head. "It doesn't wash. If you want to remind somebody of *The Raven,* you don't quote *Annabel Lee.* You quote *The Raven.*"

"If you're sane. Your psychiatrists seemed to think she's not—and I'm inclined to agree with them."

"Well, maybe so." McCallum stretched, then drained his coffee. "If you come up with any theories you like better, give me a call at the store. I'll be there till eight ayem. Meanwhile, I'll have a guy keep an eye on your girlfriend's house—just on the outside chance that Evelyn saw her address on a scrap of paper around here."

"I doubt she has Tobie's address."

"I'll bet you also doubted that she had a key to your apartment." He smiled. "It's a good thing you like being a dee-jay, Garland, 'cause you'd never make it as a cop."

Dave returned the smile. "Don't get me wrong, sarge. The more guards you put on Miss Williams, the better I'll like it."

"One'll suffice for now." He went to the door, started out, then turned back to Dave. "One more thing. Tell 'em tomorrow at the radio station that we'll be down to tap your phone. I have a hunch our girl will call tomorrow night. With luck, we'll be able to trace her."

"Roger."

McCallum again started out the door and again

turned back. "By the way, what happened to Mantovani?"

"Hey, you really do listen to the show, don't you?"

"Garland, if we had a teevee down at the station, I'd break my arm before I turned your show on. Meanwhile, for the foreseeable future I'm going to have to listen in the line of duty. So, please: play some Mantovani for me."

"Roger."

The police sergeant again started out and again turned back. "One final thing, Garland. Now that she's let herself into this joint twice with that duplicate key of hers, you will change the locks, won't you?"

"Right, sarge."

"Good. Because, Garland, the next time you may not be so lucky—and I'd hate for the guys down at the station to have to chip in and buy a teevee."

This time he really did leave.

SEVENTEEN

"A golden oldie," enthused Al Monte, "from the year nineteen hundred and sixty-three. And tell me, momma, did you ever think you'd hear anybody speak of sixty-three as the good old days?" He bled in his theme. "Ah, well, time marches on—and it's time for your pal Al to march on outta here, too. Warming up in the bullpen, babies, is that olden goldie himself, the Big D, dashing and dapper Dave Garland, all set to tuck you in with five hours of mellow groove. So, sweet people, till the morrow, 'tis the stallion heah, and you-all stay right theah. Heah? Heah, heah!"

He flicked off the microphone, then went to the table where Sergeant McCallum and another policeman were testing their phone tap equipment. Dave stood behind them, watching.

"It's all yours, daddy," Al said, gesturing toward the console. "Your theme is cued up."

"Thanks, babes." Dave crossed to the console with a book of poetry, which he opened to a premarked page and propped up next to the mike.

"How's the Tobe?" Al asked.

"Holding up fine. I spoke to her just a few minutes ago. I'm going over after the show. Meanwhile, she and her new roommate are going to stay home and do some work on a hooked rug or something like that."

"I'll gladly baby sit during the show, if you like." He did a Groucho Marx thing with his eyes. "Who knows? The new roomie might be a pretty baby. You see her yet?"

"No. Anyway, McCallum has a stake-out on the place. But thanks anyway."

"Want me to stay here with you? Just in case?"

Dave clapped him on the shoulder. "Thanks, babes. I think we have it all under control." He turned back to the console and, as the second hand on the studio clock crossed the twelve, cut Monte's theme and touched the switch triggering the taped call-letters announcement. Then, bleeding in his own theme, he turned on the mike and read,

"Once upon a midnight dreary, while I pondered, weak and weary,

"Over many a quaint and curious volume of forgotten lore—

"While I nodded, nearly napping, suddenly there came a tapping,

"As of someone gently rapping, rapping at my chamber door—
"Only this and nothing more . . .

"Open here I flung the shutter, when, with many a flirt and flutter
"In there stepped a stately Raven of the saintly days of yore.
"Not the least obeisance made he; not a minute stopped or stayed he;
"But, with mien of lord or lady, perched above my chamber door—
"Perched upon a bust of Pallas just above my chamber door—
"Perched, and sat, and nothing more . . .

" 'Prophet!' said I, 'thing of evil!—prophet still, if bird or devil!
" 'By that Heaven that bends above us—by that God we both adore
" 'Tell this soul with sorrow laden if, within the distant Aidenn,
" 'It shall clasp a sainted maiden whom the angels name Lenore—
" 'Clasp a rare and radiant maiden whom the angels name Lenore.'
"Quoth the Raven, 'Nevermore.' "

" 'Be that word our sign of parting, bird or fiend!' I shrieked, upstarting—

"'Get thee back into the tempest and the Night's Plutonian shore!

"'Leave no black plume as a token of that lie thy soul hath spoken!

"'Leave my loneliness unbroken—quit the bust above my door!

"'Take thy beak from out my heart, and take thy form from off my door!'

"Quoth the Raven, 'Nevermore.' . . .

"And the Raven, never flitting, still is sitting, still is sitting

"On the pallid bust of Pallas just above my chamber door,

"And his eyes have all the seeming of a demon's that is dreaming,

"And the lamp-light o'er him streaming throws his shadow on the floor;

"And my soul from out that shadow that lies floating on the floor

"Shall be lifted—nevermore!"

Dave held a long beat of silence, then said quietly into the mike, "Spooky thoughts for a foggy night. My name is Dave Garland and for the next five hours I'm going to try to dispel the gloom with some sensuous sounds for sensuous people. Here's Ella Fitzgerald."

He cut his theme with one hand, while with the other he started the record on Turntable One. As Ella's rendition of the Rogers and Hart classic, *Bewitched*, activated the red needle on the sound level meter, the light on one of the phones began flashing.

"KRML," he said, "Dave Garland."

"Hi, darling," said Evelyn Draper. "Was that *Raven* recitation for me?"

He gestured to McCallum that it was she on the line. McCallum replied by moving one hand in circles—keep her talking as long as possible. The other policeman rapidly went to work trying to trace the call before she hung up.

"I thought you'd like it," Dave said into the phone. "Remember that night when you quoted *The Raven* to me?"

"Of course."

"You know, Evelyn, I always meant to ask you but never got around to it: how'd you know *The Raven* was my favorite poem?"

"I didn't, actually. But I knew Poe was your favorite poet. That's hardly a secret, darling, to someone who listens to your show regularly."

"And you are a regular listener, aren't you? Tell me, Evelyn—I never thought of asking you this before either, I guess—when was the first time you—" He broke off as the connection suddenly went dead. He wheeled to McCallum. "Did you cut us off?"

"No," replied the policeman at the table. "I think she hung up. Before I could trace it, too, damn it."

McCallum shrugged. "You were pretty obvious in the way you were stalling, Garland. She probably suspected something."

"Sure—she learned all about tracing a call when she studied at the police academy." He smirked. "She's not a master criminal, McCallum. She's a crazy chick."

"And you're a lousy straight man. Try harder when she calls again—which should be any second now."

Angry with McCallum for needling him and angrier with himself for deserving it, Dave turned back to the console and cued up a Miles Davis album. The phone was flashing. He answered it hopefully. No luck. The caller was a teenaged boy who wanted to hear a new Charlie Mingus tune.

Dave played three more cuts and took eight more phone calls, all without luck. Then Evelyn called again.

"You were trying to stall me, David. Are the cops there with you trying to trace the call?"

"Yeah, they're right here, Evelyn. Would you like to speak to Sergeant McCallum?"

"Tell them to save their time, David. They're not going to trace the call." Again the line went dead.

"Not a master criminal, eh, Garland?" said McCallum. "Just a crazy chick!"

"Okay," Dave murmured. "I'm eating crow. Meanwhile, what do I do if she calls again?"

"Just keep trying to hold her. I've got the feeling that she's going to keep calling and calling. We'll just hang on and hope you can catch her with her guard down."

Dave took two more calls and played another cut. Then Evelyn placed her third call.

"Listen carefully, David, because I'm going to say it only once. *This was the reason that, long ago, in this kingdom by the sea, a wind blew out of a cloud, chilling my beautiful Annabel Lee.* Tobie Williams dies tonight, David." Click.

He turned, ashen-faced, to McCallum.

"Don't panic," said the police sergeant. "Evelyn's up against more than she probably realizes. My man is out there watching your girl's house. I'll get to him on the squad car radio and tell him about the threat. He'll see to it that no one gets inside."

"How about having him wait inside with the girls? To make extra-sure nothing happens."

McCallum shook his head. "The only way we're going to catch Evelyn is by giving her enough room to make a move. If she gets there and sees a squad car parked in the driveway, she'll just turn away."

"He doesn't exactly have to park in the driveway, does he?"

"I don't even want to take the chance of her seeing him enter the house. So he stays outside until she makes a move—if she makes a move. Meanwhile, I'll go there myself and double up with him. Don't worry —there's no way anyone will get past us. Now give Tobie a call to put your mind at ease that she's all right. And if you feel like it, call her every hour or so until you go off the air—although I think it might be a good idea not to alarm her needlessly by telling her about the threat. There's not too much she can do other than just sit there and wait."

Dave nodded, then dialed Tobie's number. He felt some of his tension leave when she answered with a cheery hello.

"Hi, honey," he said. "Just checking in. Everything all right?"

"Marvelous. We just finished up with the rug. Now I'm getting ready to do my nails. Got your show on. You seem a little nervous."

"Yeah. I guess I will be until they have her behind bars."

"Well, don't worry on my account. The doors and windows are all locked and I feel safe as a bug in a rug—or something like that."

"Where's what's-her-name—your roommate?"

"Annabelle? In the kitchen building a couple of coffee grogs. She's being wonderful about the whole thing. If I were in her place, I think I'd've checked out as soon as I learned what was up."

"You told her?"

"Only that you'd been attacked and that you didn't think Evelyn knew my name or address. Anyway, she's been just great about it. Mothering me like a hen. And she said to tell you she'll have a nice steaming coffee grog waiting for you when you get here."

"Tell her light on the coffee and heavy on the grog. And ask her her favorite song. I might as well play something for the two of you, as long as you're listening."

He waited while Tobie called to her roommate and received a reply. "She said," Tobie reported, "that she likes everything you play. Just make it soft and dreamy."

"Gotcha." On his memo pad he wrote, "Soft and dreamy. Tobie and Annabelle." Then he hung up and took a Stan Kenton album from the playrack. As he cued it he found himself staring at his note and wondering why he suddenly had such a strange feeling of foreboding.

EIGHTEEN

Tobie Williams replaced the receiver in its cradle and gazed up at the portrait of Dave over her mantel. She felt good about him now. So good. All the doubts and suspicions she had entertained were gone. Once this nonsense with that crazy girl was over, there would be no more obstacles in his and her path: they would move in together and things would be the way she had always dreamed.

"Here we are."

Tobie looked up with a smile as her new roommate came in from the kitchen carrying two steaming mugs. The girl was an absolute gem! What a shame Tobie hadn't been able to find someone like her back in the days when she had no plans to move in with David.

"I hope you like cinnamon in yours."

Tobie took the mug, touched it to her lips, then

smacked them approvingly. "Delicious. Annabelle, you're too good for words."

"So's this." She gestured toward the portrait above the mantel. "I've admired it from the moment I saw it."

"Why, thank you."

"Just one thing. You don't mind?"

"Be my guest."

"The eyes. They're wrong."

"You think? What's wrong with them?"

"David's are more—I don't know—colder."

Tobie looked up from her mug, startled. "I didn't realize you knew Dave."

"Know him?" Evelyn Draper smiled. "Not really. No more than he knows me, really."

Tobie Williams felt a paralyzing chill as her eyes followed her new roommate across the room. Tobie could not say how she knew; but at that moment, she knew.

Evelyn Draper went to the sewing table where they had been working on their hooked rug. She smiled at Tobie and knew from Tobie's expression that Tobie had finally caught on.

"Well, pussycat," she said, chuckling, "it took you longer than it should have but not as long as I thought it would. Evidently you're not as dumb as you act."

She picked up the gleaming silver scissors on the sewing table and briskly tested it in the air.

NINETEEN

Dave cued up Stan Kenton's *Lush Life* on Turntable One, then faded the volume on Turntable Two and switched on the mike. "Nine forty-five and very foggy. Now here's something soft and dreamy for Tobie and Annabelle."

Annabelle! ! !

The name reverberated through his head like a fierce Jimi Hendrix swipe-chord.

How could he have been so stupid? How could he have missed so many obvious clues?

Frantically he dialed Tobie's number. The phone rang twice, five times, ten.

He stared numbly at the receiver for a second, then slammed it into its cradle. "Get McCallum and the stakeout man on their car radios," he told the policeman at the table. "Tell them Evelyn Draper is in Tobie's house, posing as her roommate."

He dashed into the adjacent office, rummaged through the big drawer in the side of his desk, and produced the tape he had recorded months earlier in anticipation of a quick trip to San Francisco. He hurriedly threaded it into the tape recorder on the console, then hand-wound the tape past his opening chatter. When *Lush Life* ended, he flicked on the tape.

"The year is nineteen thirty-eight," his voice came through the overhead monitor, "the place Carnegie Hall, the band Benny Goodman, the trumpet Ziggy Elman—what else but, *And the Angels Sing*?"

He again dialed Tobie's number. This time it was answered on the first ring.

"We're waiting for you, David," said Evelyn Draper.

The line clicked dead in his ear.

He dashed out of the studio, bounded into his MG and roared out of his parking place.

TWENTY

"Kneel," said Evelyn Draper, holding the scissor points inches from Tobie Williams' face.

Somewhere deep inside her brain a voice was telling Tobie to disobey, put up a fight now or she'd never get another chance. But the scissor points were gleaming in front of her eyes and she knew that Evelyn would not hesitate to use them. She knelt.

"Put your hands behind your back," Evelyn said.

"Why are you doing this?"

"Behind your back!" Evelyn feinted at Tobie's face with the scissors. Its points almost touched the flesh beneath Tobie's eyes.

Tobie put her hands behind her back.

Evelyn took a ball of twine from the sewing table and tightly bound Tobie's wrists. "I'm doing it," she said after a moment, "because that arrogant son of a bitch you call your boyfriend deserves to be taught a lesson." She chuckled hollowly. "No—actually I'm doing it because I've had a lifelong desire to get back at my mother for balling my father. Anyway, that's what the shrinks that examined me think."

Her chuckle became a laugh with a fiendishly maniacal edge to it. "Actually," she said in a low, even tone, which contrasted sharply with the laugh and became all the more menacing because of the contrast, "I don't know why I'm doing it. I'm doing it, I suppose, because I feel like it. Now no more questions."

She took a kerchief from the sewing table and used it as a gag. Then she led Tobie to the couch and gestured for her to lie down. She tied Tobie's feet, then turned her onto her side so that she could see the portrait over the mantel.

Evelyn brought a chair to the fireplace, climbed up, took down the portrait and leaned it against the fireplace, facing Tobie. "These eyes," she said reprovingly, "they're not right—not right at all. They'll just have to go." She touched a scissor tip to one eye and pushed through the canvas, then did the same with the other eye.

"And the nose. It's all wrong. Not on the picture, mind you. On the human being—if he can be called a human being. It's a little boy's nose; a cute nose. He shouldn't have a nose like that. Because he's a mean and heartless son of a bitch." She poked one scissor tip through the canvas, then very carefully cut the nose from the portrait.

"And that mouth. It's so deceiving. You hear his lovely voice and you think he's a warm and sensitive person who's capable of the most profound love—a love like Poe's for his lost Lenore, his Annie, his Annabel. Ha! This man isn't capable of love. This man is a fake. He reads poems—but he feels nothing."

She cut the mouth from the portrait, then stepped back and regarded the mutilated painting appraisingly. "I hate this man!" she screamed suddenly. "I hate this rotten son of a bitch more than I've ever hated anyone! I hate this son of a bitch to death!"

She slashed at the portrait with the scissors, carving huge gashes in the canvas. Soon the entire center had been slashed through, leaving only strips of canvas which hung from the edges of the frame and fell out of range as she lunged at them. In a burst of fury she kicked over the painting, then picked it up and smashed the frame against the fireplace.

Now she turned to Tobie Williams and her fury was suddenly replaced by cold, patient hate. "Your turn," she said softly.

Tobie shrank back as Evelyn lay the cold blade of the scissors against Tobie's cheek. Evelyn chuckled hollowly at the helpless girl's expression of horror and teasingly began to rake the scissor points over Tobie's face.

"I'll bet David loves your eyes," she said, letting the scissor tips hover over Tobie's eyes like two bees poised over flowers.

Tobie winced almost involuntarily and Evelyn, chuckling fiendishly, feinted with the scissor tips. "You'd better be careful, pussycat. If I get angry, I'll put both your eyes out and make you eat them."

She lifted the scissors and stepped back to contemplate Tobie's face. "Ah, yes, such lovely eyes—especially when you're frightened—as you now are. And such lovely blonde hair. I'll bet David just loves your hair. Does he run his fingers through these pretty locks?"

She held up a tuft of hair, then snipped it off. This seemed to set something off inside her, because all of a sudden her old fury returned and she began hacking away at Tobie's hair as wildly as she had slashed at the painting. "Have to get you all nice for David!" she screamed, tears streaking down her cheeks. "I hope he likes what he sees when he walks in here—because that's the vision he's taking to hell with him!"

She continued to cut until Tobie's scalp had been all but denuded. Then she stepped back and, smiling maniacally, contemplated her handiwork. "Ah, yes, David is going to have a real sight in store for him tonight—"

She broke off as she heard a sound on the porch. She listened for a moment, heard it again, then backed to one side of the door.

There was a knock on the door. Evelyn waited silently.

"Miss Williams?" called Sergeant McCallum.

Evelyn said nothing.

"Miss Williams—open up, please. I have a telegram for you."

Evelyn remained silent.

McCallum knocked and called several times more, then was quiet. Evelyn heard his footsteps and those of another man on the porch.

"That stupid policeman," she said softly to Tobie. "Did he actually expect me to believe he was a Western Union boy? Doesn't he realize I knew David would call the fuzz?"

She went to her purse, took out a small, pearl-handled revolver and checked the ammunition. Then she set up a lamp on the floor so that its shade aimed a spotlight-like cone of light at the door. This accomplished, she went to the terrace doors overlooking the ocean, checked their locks, and opened the drapes that covered the adjacent picture windows.

"Miss Williams," called Paul McCallum, "this is the police. Open the door immediately, please, or I'm going to have to break it open."

"Break it open, flatfoot," Evelyn said too softly for him to hear. Quickly but calmly, she pulled a chair into place on the dark side of the lamp on the floor and turned off all the other lights in the room. Then she sat in the chair and released the safety on her revolver.

Paul McCallum shot open the lock and kicked the door in. Evelyn Draper smiled as she saw him and his subordinate framed in the doorway; they could not have been more perfect targets.

She pulled the trigger six times and the two policemen fell to the floor.

She calmly went to her purse and reloaded the revolver.

TWENTY-ONE

"Eight-oh-seven p.m.," Dave heard his own voice say—inaccurately—through the car radio, "and I'm Dave Garland. Here's a pretty tune for lonely lovers on a foggy night: Errol Garner and *Misty*. This is especially for Evelyn. Music to say farewell by."

He leaned over the wheel of the speeding MG, peering into the thick fog. Suddenly he spotted the mailbox he was looking for, jerked the wheel, and skidded to a halt in Tobie Williams' driveway.

He bounded up the walk and took the front stairs two at a time. Then he stopped in his tracks and felt his knees threaten to give way beneath him as he saw McCallum and the other dead policeman lying in pools of blood in the doorway.

He leaped off the porch and ran around to the catwalk separating the house from the balcony that overlooked the palisades. The drapes were open and through the big picture window he could see the strangely lit living room. The lamp on the floor cast weird shadows against the walls. The room seemed empty. He tried the door, found it locked, and moved down the catwalk to the bedroom.

Here all the lights were off, but there was enough natural illumination from outside for Dave to make out the form in the chair next to the picture window. Evelyn Draper was sitting there guarding the bed where Tobie lay bound and gagged.

Dave quietly made his way back to the front of the house. Stepping gingerly over the bodies of McCallum and the other policeman, he tiptoed through the living room. He paused outside the open bedroom door for a moment, then burst into the room and threw himself at the chair next to the picture window—only to find it empty.

Suddenly Evelyn Draper was on top of him, driving her scissors downward. He had started to turn the second he was aware of her, but didn't get out of the way in time. One blade of the scissors tore into his thigh, just below the groin and he doubled over in pain as Evelyn leaped back into the darkness.

The scissors still embedded in his flesh, he struggled to his feet and managed to stagger after her into the living room. He lost her in the shadows, then heard a scuffling to one side of him and whirled around, only to get stabbed again—this time by a knife in the shoulder.

She drew the knife away and again disappeared into the darkness. He took two steps toward her, then dropped to his knees.

Again she leaped at him, slicing out with her knife. He tried to grab the handle, but she drew away too quickly. His hand closed around the blade, and he pulled back in agony as he felt his fingers being cut through to the bone.

His legs now were like soft rubber. He wobbled forward on his knees, then pitched over onto his side.

Evelyn stood above him, the knife pointed at his throat. "Are you ready to die, you son of a bitch?" she asked evenly.

He felt his brain go numb as he struggled fiercely to hold on to consciousness. He could feel the hot blood flowing stickily from his wounds, coagulating in the fibers of his clothes.

He measured his distance from her. Her ankle was about two feet from his hand. If he lunged quickly enough, or if she stepped closer, he might just be able to catch her off balance.

"Well, you're not going to die yet," she continued. "First you're going to watch pussycat die. Now get up and come with me."

He lay motionless, waiting for her to react to his lack of reaction.

"Get up!" she repeated sharply.

He remained still and held his breath, ready to spring.

"Do you hear me? I said get up!" She took a step

toward him, then another. Then, suddenly, she kicked out at him—and he grabbed her foot.

She wasn't prepared for his resistance. She staggered back, bumped into a chair, then regained her balance —just as he got to his feet and charged her. His shoulder caught her in the waist, like a football lineman's block, driving her backward.

She struggled to get out of his way, then suddenly pitched backward as her feet hit the lamp she had set up on the floor. Dave felt her fall away from him and stared incredulously as she windmilled against the picture window, through it, onto the balcony and over the railing of two-by-fours.

As his fogging brain pieced together what was happening, he found himself remembering that day long ago when he stood on the balcony and wondered what it would feel like to plummet over the edge . . .

Probably you'd hang in space for a moment that seemed like forever; then you'd hurtle toward the rocks, down, down, watching them grow larger and larger as they drew nearer and nearer . . . then, *Splat!* A monstrous black-gray rock covered with blood and flesh and shattered bone . . .

Evelyn Draper's body was still lying on the rocks the next morning when Dave and Tobie returned from the hospital where his wounds had been dressed. He stood on the balcony and looked down at her and, as a faint breeze began to rustle through her chestnut hair, it occurred to him that her face seemed as innocent as a child's in the misty morning sunlight.